SOME DIFFERENT
EDEN

A NOVEL BY PATRICK DWYER

ICE HOUSE
PRESS

SOME DIFFERENT EDEN

"This is the part where I tell you that all similarities to actual events or to the living or the dead are coincidental.

"I wish it were true."

One

He is looking at me with an easy concentration. With patience. Waiting. Like he knows me. Like I know what he wants.

I don't.

He seems familiar though, his hair dark and short, his eyes the same color and almond-shaped. Like I must have seen him before, maybe many times.

From my bench across from him, everything around me begins to slide out of focus. Except for the boy.

He gets clearer.

I think I do remember him. I think … I think I met him, long ago. In another country. Another me.

Why is he here, now? How can he still be the same boy? He would be a man now, if he was still alive — which did not seem likely at the time.

1

_/_/ 2007. The Present.

I am not looking both ways.

I have been dwelling on 'Purpose' again. Working myself up. Feeling the hot wires running from my heart, down the insides of my arms, to my fingertips.

I know I am not supposed to give in to this.

I step off the curb, stumbling, glaring up at the towering skyline. I know it's there, I know what it looks like. Even when it's obscured by lowering mists on an endless afternoon drizzle. Purpose, I think, my molars crunching, the 'purpose' we are all supposed to have. Purpose that places wealth above everything. Like these buildings are above everything, and everyone.

My angry thoughts are ripped back to the right now blare of horns, screech of tires, oncoming grillwork and headlights of a giant SUV, and I am frozen in the middle of the street with my death approaching, eyes staring, sightless ...

Dark brown eyes reflecting bitter
points of light, beneath conical dark
hats ... heart-stopping sound of
bullets passing too close,

*impenetrable dark greenery
spouting its own deadly points of
light …*

Then.

Sight.

I am down. But not on a city street.

I jerk upright, seizing my breath like it's my last, arms outstretched to some distant salvation.

I'm not dead!

I stop, staring, rigid. My head! Am I hit?

I am sitting in sand, surrounded by sand. And by tough men in desert camo, and one of them's got my arm in his.

There are words buzzing in my head, and the guy holding my arm is mumbling something at me, something supposed to be soothing, I can tell, but there is no sound – until it all suddenly rushes in. Gunfire, a lot of it, close by. The din and smoke of combat.

I know this sound, this smell! The tough men are running everywhere, yelling, some taking firing positions.

The words of the man next to me come clear, "Charlie, you alright buddy? Are you hit? Jeez you just keeled over, scared the shit out of me!"

I know this man, I know I like him a lot. Borden. No, Burton. The corpsman!

"Come on Charlie, snap out of it! Are you hit? You look dazed. Are you alright? Jeez, we got incoming Charlie, look alive!"

Incoming. In a desert? No! And I'm wearing the same gear as the rest of them? This can't be – I can't be here!

I pull my arm free of Burton's grip, get a knee under myself, scrunch my neck at the sound of an explosion just off to the right, instinctively grab my pot and snap it on my head as a rain of sand sifts down on us. "Jesus! Burton? What the fuck?" I shout, looking for and picking up my weapon and running with him to join the squad.

Rounds are coming from everywhere, rocket explosions rattle the insides of my head, add their arrhythmic pulse to my own. Everything whirls crazily, vertigo knots my guts.

If this were jungle or grassy plains, I could just be dreaming!

I see no target opportunities, no enemy visible to me. I am not even firing my weapon! There's a quick swell to the small arms fire, topped by two more nearby explosions ... then nothing. Floating, I struggle to breathe.

I lie on my back on the sand, still spinning, unable to touch down. The sun hurts my eyes, and I'm not even looking at it.

And I'm stuck to the inside of my gear, sweat running into my boots.

What am I saying?

I'm dead. I am lying on the street. This is my hell.

No. I know where I am. Iraq. Al Anbar Province. And I'm talking to myself. Charles Artemis Bird, United States Marines.

I'm having some kind of psychotic break. Again. Too much stored up. I'm no Marine, I'm a Vietnam army vet. A medic. Was a medic. Just a bitter old man now. But I have the same name here? Charles Artemis Bird?

What is happening to me? I know this place, this fucking desert. I know these Marines. What am I listening to, inside me? I'm cracking up.

They say it happens.

You can't think about having a psychotic break inside of a psychotic break. This is desert, not jungle. And it's way too real to be a dream. My blood hasn't hammered through my body like this, the strength in my guts ... since I was young, and before ... .

I AM young! STOP IT! Of course it's a goddamn desert, it's not a dream! I wish maybe it was. I scramble up.

We move on, reach our objective. A village harboring suspected rebels, maybe the same ones we just shot it out with. The white walls of the nearby buildings here on the outskirts are more painful in the unrelenting light than they've been since I got here. We take a break and I open a pouch of rations, look inside. Sniff at it. Ugh.

They were always terrible.

I stick my fork into the glop and lift out a bite and my head swims, like the worst kind of sea sickness. I barely feel the fork drop from my numb fingers into the sand, the shimmering walls start a sideways dance, and my insides heave in a rush to escape my suddenly yawning mouth. I fall. And drift ...

"Our brother lies there," she says, her luminous eyes fixed on mine, her left arm pointing up the gully. She is lit from behind by a westering winter

*sun. All I can distinguish in her face
are those eyes …*

I come to with my cheekbone aching where it is pressed to the pavement, my eyes inches from the enormous tire tread of the SUV that has run me down. I am lying in the street curled on my side, hearing nothing, mentally probing to see how badly I am hurt.

No gully. No desert. Not war.

I'm back.

From where?

Road smells, tar, heavy crude, fill my nostrils, a rising murmur of voices in my ears. Now sirens and car horns. Then, pain. Everywhere.

My whole body is suddenly wracked in spasms, and I lash out in fury, "m m mm aaa aahh – mah ahh – gg ahh gah ah – muh guhh guh," I hear myself stutter, my cry stifled. 'My gun!' I'm trying to yell. 'Give me my gun! You bastards! I'll kill you all!' But all that gets past my rattling teeth is, "Yyuh unh uhh!" The foam of my anger spilling down my cheek to pool at my ear on the pavement.

"Easy! No! Don't straighten him out! Just hold his head straight, get this into his teeth!" Someone yells into a growing distance, my forehead beginning now to slap the asphalt in a rhythm that fades into nothing.

Sunlight streaming through upturned blinds. I can hear far below the audible breath of the city and the cry of gulls. I turn my head to see a face. Diagonal bars of light cross her cheeks, her nose. *Her*? Here? How can it be?

"Easy Tiger!" She chides, the humor in her voice undisguised. "You had us pretty worried." She puts down a small tray and tucks in a corner of my bedding and sternly advises "Now you just relax and let the medicine do its work." But there's a trace of self-mockery there.

She turns to look at something above my bed, and the bars of light slide off her. She is so young, too young. I see that. And it was so long ago. Thirty years? More? What did I just see? First the desert, then me as roadkill? Then ... her?. But not *'her'*. "You ... ," I manage, but can find no words to continue.

"Me," she replies. "Yes, well ... me. But I don't think I'm the 'me' you want. I just have that effect on people. Especially when they wake up from near death and what the chart here says was an epileptic seizure." She moves closer to regard my face. "You sure look like you been through the war − in a manner of speaking. Maybe you just better rest quiet, catch your breath, catch up. Something like this leaves folks feeling pretty, well, emptied out − I hear."

No, it's not her. Not ... the nurse I first thought. Maybe wanted to think, needed to think. Why now, why would I need to think that now? She's very nice. Like that other nurse ... after I got blown up.

She's looking at me. Is that recognition? I'm in no shape to make guesses. She's a nurse, she's supposed to look at me. And she's right. I do feel emptied out. I've got nothing left to talk with right now. I'm so tired I can hardly see. A breeze ripples curtains and I float. Bees buzz, mumble, my head separates in the warm broth. It's coming, the dream. I can feel it. I can't stop it. A sharp slide down and a bump. Then nothing … .

Sounds and images of war in the jungle stir crazily, broken off from any reality they ever might have had. A mortar round crashing nearby is muted to almost nothing, the flash and heat of it only flickering like cozy firelight … haze from napalmed vegetation drifts like woodsmoke … wiffs of leaking vitality are sterilized to hospital freshness … the shouting, all the awful screams, distant, a mere historical footnote. The pulse of rotors comes directly overhead and every organ in my body leaps in rhythm and throbs to dance in the gyre, and day and night start alternating like a trick scene in a movie. And the lights and knives of surgery. And more surgery. And a rocket ship ride strapped to the fuselage interior of a giant cargo bay, tubing running into me. Everywhere, into me… .

The same dream I had, I think I had, that I woke from on a morning … long ago.

• • •

A morning that comes and I am awake, and I know pretty much who I am, or was. What is left of me is partially sitting up in bed, surrounded only by white and by the kind of order you only find in a hospital. There is no sign of jungle, or fire, or death. There is music, a song, hard to make it out. Maybe it's Charley Pride, doing "All I have to offer you is me." And I am hungry. Figures. I'm probably on a clear liquid diet and now I feel, for the first time since getting hit, that I could eat the ass out of a dead water buffalo.

A pretty nurse comes over to my plate of Jell-O with a wrinkled nose and a smile that says it all to me.

"You want it?" I offer.

She shakes her head. It makes her long hair wave below her cap, with the tips alternately brushing both sides of her chin.

"No? They made it special for me. You don't know what you're missing," I tease.

"Yes I do," she says with a conspiratorial laugh, "and your stuck with it, Mister." The smile never leaves her face. It's a good smile, a real smile.

"They say I'm gonna live – guess the local undertaker can take a day off, huh?"

"Oh yes, you are going to live, soldier. To fight another day," she comes back at me, but with her lower lip all serious and straight, like a school marm to a five year old.

"Not according to Ben Casey out there – he says I got no more fight in me."

"If a girl believed that," she laughs, " she'd be in big trouble with you – in no time flat!"

That's what I remember. That nurse. And that was thirty-seven years ago.

• • •

After my knock-down in the street, they keep me for observation in that Seattle hospital for two more days. And I don't see the young nurse again, not once. Maybe I sent her away. Made her sell her shift. Maybe lying here is making me think too much.

I haven't been in a peek-a-boo gown in ... years. Decades. How many? Not since ... the bad stretch. And that was, well, I guess I don't know anymore. And I guess I'm ok with that.

But I'm left wondering about that thing in the sand, that ... dream-that-was-not-a-dream. The other bits were dreams, or flashbacks, doesn't matter which — but feeling young like that in a desert? And fighting again? I could never dream that. That war was happening right now, somewhere conveniently out of sight of most Americans. Brave men and women were fighting for what they believed in, some of them dying. Given my own history, I have to wonder what for.

And like everybody else, I just haven't been thinking about it. And now I've been there, haven't I.

Haven't I?

I find myself wishing I could get more focused, stop the wandering. Break the bubble. But when has that ever worked out for me?

Maybe this would be different. Maybe I'm different. Now. After all this time. Maybe this time I won't go off the rails.

It makes my stomach wrench and my old wounds burn, but I can tell I am actually wondering about going back to that sand, in some awful way maybe even wanting it. I can't just keep going like it's been for me – aimless, trying to just stay out of trouble. Reading? Yes, a lot of reading. Maybe too much. And sometimes the odd writing project for one of the radical sheets in town.

So, yes, maybe that's what that was. A wake up in the desert. War. The same damn war that I had fought nearly 40 years ago. Wasn't it. That nearly killed me, that did kill so many others. And like it never happened, here it is, all over again.

Maybe it's time. Maybe I *should* say something. *Do* something … .

If I could just Not Get Crazy. Again.

2

One day not long ago I realized I had been dead for twenty years. I knew where I was. But I did not remember much of anything. I could remember only in the dimmest way what I had been doing with myself, not much better than if I had simply dreamed about two decades of living and now it was all fading with the dawn. I had done what I had to do, hadn't I? Stayed alive?

Nothing else.

Because all that time, there had been no fear, no disappointment. And no anger. Every day just came and went.

I guess I do have some recollections of living on the street. A succession of shelters. A lot of time in hospital hallways. Interviews. Group sessions. No details. I do not recall the faces of anyone. Well, hardly anyone.

I looked at myself that day. I was fit, sort of. I could walk and stand alright. And I was clean. So I guess I hadn't been sleeping in dumpsters. At least not recently. And it was all strange.

It wasn't amnesia. Just absence. Like I had left and sublet the building for 20 years. Only it seemed to me that day like I was back. Seeing the ghosts again. And living the anger.

And today, I remember. This has all happened before, more than once. Always the return of the anger. Always the longing for a violent 'episode'. And then always the flight back, into being mostly dead.

Well, I guess I've had my last retreat. There'll be no more sleeping wakefulness.

Charles Artemis Bird, Man with a Purpose? We'll see.

• • •

"Artemis, here's one for you." He thinks he's Perry White sometimes, King of the Scoop. I got my clothes on and came right over from the hospital to tell him I didn't want any more filler pieces for his rag. Instead, and without looking up from the piles on his desk, Prisker hands me a folder with some clippings attached to the outside of it.

"Guy named Ray." Lifting his glasses and pulling the folder back to read, he adds, "Clayton Ray." He holds the folder out to me again and continues, "Was a Black activist back in the 60's. Anti-war, the whole deal. Now he's doing the full nine on Murder Deuce in California at a minimum security prison they call Camp Snoopy down there." He stops talking when he notices he's still holding the folder, drops his glasses back down on his nose, and waives the folder impatiently at me until I take it from him. He looks at me like I know the answer he's been waiting for all day.

This is not what I came in here for. I don't want some human interest nostalgia! I want to get in someone's face, call down the Gods! The heat is just beginning to run down the insides of my arms, my guts starting to twist. I want to throw the folder at him! And then throw myself across the desk and … !

"Do we all need to take a nice chill pill?" he asks softly, looking in my face, and knowing what he is looking at. I hold still. "I see you got your eye on something else. That's ok with me," he shrugs. "You know where that goes, right? Back on the street? Or worse?" He is looking meaningfully at my clenched right hand, the folder edges crumpled in my left.

I look at the folder in my hand. "Okay," I admit. And the heat goes out of me. He's right. I've just lost it right off the bat, out of control already and I haven't even started in.

"Ok," he says, like we are done with that, and looks back down at the stuff on his desk.

I straighten out the edges of the folder, uncrumple one of the clippings, and take a seat in the corner, flipping randomly through what he's given me. "So? What's this?"

"That's what I want you to tell me. Find out about him. What's he doing. What's he like. Now. Is he still a flaming radical?"

"Why California?" I study his face for what he won't be telling me.

He gives me his 'what you don't know about the newspaper business' smirk. "Why not. Folks around here have a morbid fascination with anything California. You know that. Besides, he has a sister lives up here now. That's what she says. Find out about her too. Good looker. Can't be half his age. Sat in that chair right there," he points to the one in front of his desk, the one I am not sitting in, never sit in. "She gave me the clippings, said she likes the paper, said we could make a good story out of it."

"Your kidding." He is definitely not telling me everything.

"No. I'm not. But I think she might have been. See what you can find out – usual deal. I agree with her though – I do think it will make a good story for our readers, maybe even a short series? How about that?"

'Usual deal' with Prisker means I work my ass off and get paid barely expenses. But then I don't need much, and he seems to think I am good at this kind of thing. A nice co-dependency that way. "Ok," I tell him, unclipping the notes and putting them inside the folder and standing up. "Did she leave an address or number?"

"Yeah, it's in with the notes. Need an advance on expenses?"

"No. I'm good." I turn and walk to the door of his office.

"Hey." He says to my back, "She asked for you by name."

That stops me, but I do not turn around. Then I notice I've stopped and I get going. I feel side-tracked. But I like the idea. Maybe this will be the springboard for what I need to be saying. Besides, how could anyone know my name?

The notes tell me Ray is in CMC (California Men's Colony) at San Luis Obispo, sometimes called Camp Snoopy or just plain San Luis Obispo. Ray was convicted of second degree attempted murder of some guy in a bar in LA 7 or 8 years ago. The notes say that the guards mostly like him and he has never been in any trouble on the inside, so he is in the West (level II) population. One note says he was offered a plea for 2-4 on ADW or aggravated assault, but turned it down and was then tried instead for second degree attempted murder and got a max sentence of nine years.

There's more in the file about his post war treatments, episodes of PTSD, his military service which ended with him getting acquitted of a double fragging homicide on his base in Vietnam in 1970. That's when I was there too. Maybe even the same place. I almost remember, or think I remember, about two lieutenants dying that way, about that time. Maybe I'm making that part up. But I want to meet the sister, if that's who she is, and hear it from her.

She lives in Monroe, near the river, and not far from the state prison there. I borrow a car for the drive up, and after some asking around, I find her address easily enough. But I am not prepared for what happens to me when she answers the door.

She is the most beautiful woman I have ever seen.

Not like magazines or movies. Like a real person. And somehow I feel like I already know her. Well, not really of course – but there is some kind of deep connection, or something, instantly. I can see her own eyes, incredible, delicate, slightly almond-shaped eyes, I can see them widen, and her own breath catch. Like mine. And it is not ... well, she is barely in her twenties, and I'm not ... well, I haven't been with anyone in a long time, and I'm not attracted to her, not that way. I hear the word 'stunned' applied sometimes, and that is what it is for me. I am stunned. This is not Ray's sister. Not his sister. She's ...

"He is my grandfather, Mr. Bird," she says, as if in answer to my thoughts. "Will you come in? I have some tea for us. I have been looking forward to meeting you."

3

Iraq. Al Anbar Province.
_/_/2007. The Present.

The stupid rug.

The rug they took from that house in the village that we burned down.

I didn't want to take it. They wanted it. Blake said it was ours. It was ours now. He said the Hajis wouldn't be needing it anymore.

We were all amped up, wired to the eyeballs on combat adrenaline, equal parts of fear and anger still burning along our nerves, from the roots of our hair to our toes and fingertips. I already knew by this time this is where the bad stuff could happen, if it was going to happen. Our platoon leader nowhere in sight. Just five of us from the squad. There'd been six of us to start. Now we were five – could've been three. Or two. Or none. In that fight? Do you have any idea how the bottom drops out in a fight like that? Everything, and I mean everything, is up for grabs. Time stops working right. The laws of physics don't apply. Everyone is your enemy. Everyone and everything wants to kill you and your buddies. You move through thickness and pain, and sounds don't match up with what's happening. Your breath is sucked away to somewhere else. Some other dimension that you hope you can reach in time before you die in here. This bubble of death.

And when that bubble bursts, and you look around you, and you see anything standing that even *might* have just been shooting at you or blowing you up? You gun it down. Some guys do. I don't know. It hasn't happened to me yet. I'm afraid it will. I think it's only a matter of time.

So. Nobody's getting gunned down right then, and I wasn't going to be the one to stick up for a stupid rug. I just wanted to get it Over With. Get out, see if Briggs made it. Get him to aid, if he did. Get out of this place, this wreckage. Before I could start to think about people living here, loving their children ... .

Now our squad carries this rug everywhere. Not into combat of course. But everywhere the unit goes, every fire base, they bring it along, Blake and Rivers. I feel like taking it and, well, getting rid of it. Except there's no where to throw it, at least no where I could stomach throwing it. Those guys would shit if I did that, and if Blake found out it was me did it? He'd have murder in his eye. Is that sick? Or what. Only now, I think it is bringing us bad luck, instead of the good luck the rest of the guys think it brings.

The last two times we've moved base, the atmosphere around us has gotten worse. More night incidents, more IED shit. For openers. And we've got a new Lieut. Fresh out of some tin can. Not a clue about the desert. This desert. It's all Mission, and Corps.

Don't get me wrong. I know my duty, I came here to fight. I would die for the Corps, or any of these jerks I fight with. But I don't have my head up my ass. And I am not sure that everything we are doing is serving our country.

And I am starting to get these weird whatchamacallits – deja vu's. Like this, or some of this, even now, what I am thinking, has happened before. Happened to me. I don't know. It's like having snapshots of someone else's memories.

4

Monroe, Washington
_/_/2007. The Present.

"He is my grandfather Mr. Bird. My grandmother told me all about him as I grew up." She pours tea. Not unlike some version of a tea ceremony. It is articulate, graceful. A sensory experience equal to the tea, which my poor tastes can still tell is excellent. "When Clayton Ray met my grandmother, she was, like so many good looking women at the time, working at a club on Tu Do Street in Saigon."

She pronounces it 'shygong' or that's what it sounds like to me, though the rest of her speech shows hardly a hint of accent.

"How old was she?" I ask.

She looks up at me through the steam from the cup she holds in both hands as if it were an augury. Her expression plainly says, 'Next?'

"I'm sorry," I stammer. "I didn't mean ... ."

"It's quite alright Mr. Bird. I am not offended. It is just not important for you to know." She studies me a little and then adds, "Besides, I have an idea you can guess. Based upon your own experience?" And gives me a little smile, with only a slight bow of her lips.

"Please, now that I have embarrassed myself in front of you, the least you can do is call me 'Charlie'?" Or Artemis, I think. The name my sister always used with me. "Or Artemis? That's what Prisker calls me. The man you met at the paper?"

"Yes," she pronounces, as if some treaty has just been ratified. "Charlie it will be." And she looks back into her tea cup, some additional knowledge of me, it seems, hidden in her glance away at that moment. Then, as if stung by an insect, she gives a little start and reaches for my cup. "Oh, I have neglected your cup. 'Charlie'?" She says, trying it out. And again the little smile.

She makes art refilling my bowl, then waiting, suspended, until I have inhaled some of the fresh steam, "Do you want to hear more?"

"Oh, yes." I say with more enthusiasm than I intended.

This time I actually get a full chuckle from her, three quick pulses that radiate through her whole body, at least the part I can see above our tea table. Three delicate bell sounds to my ears. "Very well, Charlie." And she puts down her own cup, folds the slim fingers of her hands together and lays them on the table before her cup as if completing a still life and speaks into the rising steam.

"She never saw him again. But from him she got my mother." A quick glance up to check my eyes, then back to her cup, or now a spot just in front of it. "Little Hoa Toi was dark like him, and she got trouble from that, growing up, mostly after Vietnam was 'unified.'" Now that spot seems to have gone way distant, far beneath the table, maybe far behind the time we now share. There is some time that only she measures, then she is back. "And it made her ... rebellious." And with that, she is facing me. Directly. "She became too much for my grandmother in the end, I am afraid, and when she was old enough, she met a boy who was also the child of an *Ao My*. You know the term?" She pronounces it, with a slight lilt, "Ow Me."

I know what she means. *Ao My* was a made-up term I heard long ago, but never used. I think it meant courtesan or in crude terms, prostitute. I hesitate, just a beat, but catch her gaze grow stern immediately, startlingly. This instant, among all the dangers of my past life, this is one I cannot face. She is demanding my honesty in a way I'm powerless to refuse. I nod. Then add a resolute, "Yes."

Like her mother Hoa Toi, the boy she met was *bui doi* – a 'child of the dust', an outcast.

She nods once, returns immediately to being the woman I met at the door and continues. "Yes. *Ao My*. Just like my grandmother. History repeating. You know about this?"

"I think so," I admit, feeling myself falling further under her spell.

"They too made a love child, me, though they were both too young in an old and wicked world to survive it. No one knows what happened to them. I was left with my grandmother."

She stands up from the table and begins to clear away the tea things. I don't know what to do, or say. She busies herself in silence for a while. 'No one knows what happened to them,' she's just said. To her mother. To the boy. Her biological father.

The boy.

That boy? Do I know him? My skull starts to contract, a thing I truly do not want. Not right now. I breathe, I will it to pass. I wait.

With her back to me at some task in the sink that I cannot see and suspect is only for effect, she asks, simply, "Do you know now who my other grandfather is? Charlie?"

I do know. Now. As certainly as if I could see all the events of my whole life, and all the events that have sprung from those events, and the events from those events. "Yes." I say with a simplicity I hope matches her own.

The boy was mine. Is mine. Her father. And I am her grandfather. The word tingles in my spine, brings up for me my sister Eileen, the outcast in my own early family. The family I'd thought I had only one of to run away from. Brings up for me my own grandfather... .

• • •

Henry Richard Bird. One of the leading ranchers early in Estacado county history. An earnest and visionary young man out of the mountains of Kentucky. An uncompromising, single-minded man who had come to Texas in the early 1870s and surveyed and fenced three quarter sections of land in 1877 southwest of Babylon before Estacado was officially a county. A sonovabitch like all the men he propagated including me. He brought in Hereford cattle and over the next decade bought another 20 sections of land as his family grew.

Drought, lawlessness and hard conditions had their effect, but could not stop him. And the luck he'd brought with him from the ancient mountains stayed with him, so in 1927 a minor enterprise spurred by Bird's youngest son Richard made good.

My father Richard Cleveland Bird was a true son of his father, except he was born to be a maverick. A rancher and cowhand like all of his kind, but looking for something else. After several successful oil strikes by men in other parts of West Texas in the early 1900s he persuaded his father to let him do some exploration of his own on the family land. In 1925 the elder Bird put up several sections of land as collateral for a loan the younger Bird used to start drilling. The first two attempts were failures and, as economics worsened, Grandfather stubbornly pledged more of his land for more drilling money for Richard.

Relentless, as ever, and heedless, my father started his third well with what was then the new rotary drilling equipment and in a short few months it came in and blew harder than any that had been seen in that part of the country. Dad soon had the income to pay off all of his father's pledges, and began on a hell-bent plan to drill and turn more of the family ranch land to oil production. When the old man passed away in 1931, Richard took over the ranch and oil business and while depression-bred opportunities flourished, added even more land to the family's holdings.

Bastards, all. And now me.

• • •

She is watching me intensely.

I wonder what name my son gave to this woman. *My son?* A son I can hardly imagine. Or won't. Except ... *that* boy, in the vision, with the eyes?

Another family outcast? A whole part of a dead life I had forgotten. Wanted to forget. Thought I had.

"Tuyet," she says.

"That is your name?" I ask, still following my own thoughts.

"It is hers. You know this."

I am silent in front of her certainty. My head is buzzing, and I think some of the noise is coming out my open mouth. I search her face for signs she can hear it.

"You do. You both laughed about it."

"Tuyet," I say.

I remember it means 'snow white'. I remember she was a beautiful Vietnamese girl, anything but white. And she was no Disney character. I had asked her name after our first time together. Tuyet, she told me. And we laughed.

"Better," she breathes, reading my face. "It must all come together now. Bring back the rest," she commands softly. "Bring ... *her*."

At first it is fragmented, unreal. This ... passage I pace at her insistence. There are great spurts, gouts of sensation, pain, which close the eyes of my memory, twist my present guts, send me reeling, staggering across the lowland plains of a forgotten landscape. Brought up short, diverted, again and again. Until I stand in the doorway, ancient stringed music accompanying impossibly girlish voices. Laments and excursions not meant to be understood as words – only as one of the currents of an indomitable people. *Viet Hoa*. And the smell of whiskey, and cheap beer. And sex. It is in the air I breathe when I step over the threshold. And I see her.

A woman, a young woman, apart from the rest, wearing a white *ao dai* and open-toed slippers, her hair dark and flowing back and then flipped over her right shoulder. I can read no expression in her face, her eyes. But she is reading me. She slides gracefully forward, off the stool that held her up, now shorter than when she was sitting, and moves slowly across the space between us, never taking her eyes from mine.

She speaks to me in low conversation as she advances. "You come to *beau coup* fine place, GI. *Hai Qua!* You buy me drink now? Come sit with me. Very private. You tell me Everything." And with that she reaches and takes my hand in her tiny fingers, a slow smile of surprise, I think, as she reads something in me she had not expected.

I went along. I forgot what I came for.

I had heard this all before. Any girl in any club would say mostly the same things to every GI and sailor that came in. And why not. It mostly worked. Part of me was saying loudly that this was no different. A lot of the girls were pretty, some even beautiful. Many had the knack of at least a simulation of sympathy. And there were drinks and talk, a lot of talk, mostly from the man, and then, if you wanted, or you were just not capable any longer of saying no, the private room.

I was always reserved in this setting. Did not talk much, drank little, and enjoyed the atmosphere until it was time for me to leave. No private room. I'm not a prude, surely I wasn't then. And I had all the usual urges. So I barely understood my own actions and choices. Maybe I was afraid. Stories of venereal disease, and evidence of it too, were rampant among the guys. Most treated it as some kind of combat infantry badge, openly (in words) displaying it for all to see and admire. But I wanted none of that. Besides, I was a medic – how would that look? So, yeah, maybe a bit afraid. But we had protection issued practically with every ration pack, and I always carried several with me (made great muzzle covers for stream crossings or rainy bivouacs). The rest of it, the largest part of the – what? Ok, fear. Was a mystery to me.

So we did talk, in a corner of the smoky, dim-lit room, a long time. And I had far more to drink than I knew was good for me. And she listened. I was saying to myself, all along, yeah, she knows how to do this – but I didn't care. She took in everything I told her and gave me back – I don't know. Understanding. Sadness, for me. Admiration, in very small, almost veiled pauses. And invitation. Soft, cool, slowly warming, and rising like a tide in the South China Sea. Just me, specially me. No one else.

She sat on the bed in the private room, which I do not recall going to, with my hand in those same fingers, and her face uptilted to mine, with a look of question, of suppressed need, of request. Honest request. 'Please,' I could almost hear her say. I could not resist, did not want to resist, or even delay. I knelt down in front of her, moving her hand to my cheek, I shakily put my left hand on her cheek, and bent to kiss her. Her lips met mine with a rush and she locked her arms around my neck, and she was in me, and I in her, in a tumble of legs and raised skirts and fumbled belt buckles. And we writhed to make heaven blush, our two breaths twisted together, and our hearts and bodies pulsing, pulsing. And the mounting swell and pressure and unendurable fury inside me, surging upward, like ancient crude exploding from a long buried Permian dome, driving up the well, driving, hitting air and spark, and bursting into the night with the flare of a new sun.

So, yes, I do remember. That visit, and others, when R&R permitted. I had never felt that way. I know, it happened to lots of us. The war, the sudden unreality of a private room somewhere, fear of sudden death transformed into lust for life. The ancient species imperative. But it was different for me, I told myself. Different. And I wanted to stay with this woman. Told her what I wanted. And she agreed.

When I got – injured – and swept away, back to the other unreality, to a life as a casualty of a war no one admired and many pretended was not happening? When that happened, or to be honest, somewhere along the line of it happening, I knew I could not go back. In the end, did not want to go back. There. To her. And all the rest of it.

I tell people I got killed in Vietnam, if I tell anyone anything. I died there. In so many ways I feel like I did. And I died to her. For all she knew.

I just never came back.

I was in a pain-filled, drug-fueled haze for so long I forgot almost everything about myself, a life that was now dead to me. And I never thought about her. Then, or ever. So how could I know about the boy she brought into the middle of that war, a boy who grew up between one explosion and the next. Grew up and went out on his own, his mother broken down by her trade, or broken hearted? Or both. A boy with no memory of me, the only trace of me the deep genetic song of my ancestors. A discord in his blood.

I look up, to see this young woman of the tea ceremony turned at the sink to face me, only a bare trace of vindication in her face.

"Yes," she says simply, not quite hiding her satisfaction.

"Tuyet," I say again.

"Yes."

"And it is your name too." My turn to make a leap.

"Yes."

"You knew her?" I ask, surprised at the surge of unreasonable hope I feel.

"My father named me."

Suddenly awkward, my forehead and cheeks hot, my insides squishy, caught between my lifelong reserve and this discovery of long hidden, never to be hoped for, kinship my heart can not decide.

No. My heart is certain – it is me holding back.

She reads all that. "There is no need at this point for a simple domestic scene. I am who I am. So are you. That is enough. For now."

I make a feeble half attempt to rise, step toward her, my hands and arms stuttering, fumbling.

"No." The command again. "That will come naturally, later. Or not. I did not search you out and arrange this visit for a reunion. You and I are not a family. We are fragments of one."

I am still restless, under compulsion from parts of me I thought were gone. Left behind. Dead. Like me. I must be shaking.

"Listen to me," she speaks sternly, as to a child.

I stop, sink to the chair, an unexpected calm settling around me.

"I want my two grandfathers together. I want you both to find out the paths of the journey you have taken together, but up to now separately. I want them to be made whole." She does not say, 'you owe me this,' but it could not be plainer to me. Maybe I read that in.

Maybe that is my own need.

5

CMC - San Luis Obispo
_/_/2007. The Present.

Our 'separate paths,' she said. Clayton Ray and I. Separate paths to war? To her, our granddaughter-in-common? I think about what she is asking.

I have to fly to California now, of course. That's part of it. Meet Ray, see if he will talk to me – at all. I haven't flown anywhere since ... long ago. And the thing for Prisker? 'Clayton Ray, Radical Hero'? My 'springboard'? What of that? Huh.

Find out his path, she asks me. Maybe it is all the same thing. His path, my story about him. And even if they're not the same – maybe, especially now, I need to do both.

But me? My own 'path'? A history I have worked half my life to forget? Is that even possible? Is that really what she wants from me? Now? Do I owe that to her grandmother? To myself?

History. Amidst all the strife, the beat downs, my hatred for most of my family, there was still a separate space for me. Most of the time. Sometimes me and Eileen both. I think about that now. Try it out. Can I do this? The aircraft accelerates down the runway, its engines whining for a leap into an unknowable future.

● ● ●

I wasn't that good in school. Couldn't keep my mind on the studies. But I learned reading early from my mother, read all the time. And she helped me with books, and mostly kept that from my father and my brothers. And in all the reading, there was a compulsion, I guess, to picture ancient geology, to see it moving as if in Chaplin-esque motion. Sped up. I think now, what part of my own subterranean makeup was calling to me then? What tectonics did I long to ride then, and now.

I read about, and pictured, life in a shallow sea. A single sea, covering all the earth, surrounding a single continent. Hundreds of millions of years in a shallow sea. Life abundant, teeming, in all its primitive forms, billions of life cycles, mitotic division, growth, death, settling.

Always settling.

And the vast biomass that accumulated beneath the ripples across that shallow sea. Two parts of the continental shelf beneath that sea, as it turns out, only temporarily attached to the larger land mass that would one day be the tail of South America. These two Permian flakes were twins to each other, alike in shallow-sea-ness, in settling accumulations. All this at a time when the east coast of South America was sutured to the west coast of Africa and the unborn Atlantic was a dream in the sleeping mass of a three and one half billion year-old planet.

A planet for whom life was only a very, very recent experiment. Perhaps a passing fancy.

Who knows why, or at least why right then (in geological suddenness, at least) a great molten swirl of magnetism and magma sent a great crashing blow up underneath the vast Pangaean continent to rip loose the stitches of that long suture and send the two great proto continents, Africa and South America, on their ways, ever further from each other. And at the same time, two tangential tectonic pulses broke those maverick westward and eastward chunks off and sent them both rocketing northward to their long homes.

Who could know, who would care, that these two enormous and richly furnished beds of buried life would find their journey's ends slammed up into and then under two other proto continents now also on the move, though far slower in stately motion than the two speedy rovers.

The mass to the west slipped along the margin of the Panthalassic Ocean, while Pangaea contorted and contracted and birthed herself into the map we know today. And while the bits that would settle in place to be the Central American isthmus swirled and danced and briefly departed, the southwestern coast of the North American plate was left open to such advances. And in good time the western calf came into the corral in what is now West Texas, in the region known as the Delaware Basin.

The eastern traveler slid among the shifting plates of the latter day Indian Ocean and before the swinging gate that was the Arabian Peninsula could return and block the entrance, crashed into Central Asia, pushing up the Anatolian Plateau and settling beneath the eventual valleys of the Tigris and Euphrates flowing out of that same plateau.

Two disparate boats of bounty on the high seas of an ancient world. Come to port in what are today arguably the two greatest petroleum reserves of the present age, nearly identical in latitude and now far north of the equator from beneath which they both began. All those unimaginable tons of buried organic material, worked by the pressures of their own weight, the weight of accompanying sediments, and the weight of the lands underneath which they had slid, worked by the alchemical processes of the unknown world to become, from small bits of dead matter, the vast living pools of oil and gas over which we fight today.

And how long had I been submerged, how many layers of my life had grown over me? I now keep hearing in my head, like the refrain of an old hymn, "like a Permian Reef, sunken, bursting to rise again." Where had I got that? Is it something I'd read? Or is it the call of my own tectonic collision courses. Deep burial. Transformation. Eden lost. And found?

• • •

And apart from this lifelong obsession with ancient burial? Where could a young cowhand and roughneck have ever gotten the idea of being a medic? I can't say for certain. Maybe from a long familiarity with injury. Maybe from a desire to get as far and as good away from the rangeland of my birth as I could then imagine.

For sure, when I lit out north and west from Texas, I had nothing like that in mind. At least not where I could see it. I rode my thumb up and across the deserts, over the passes and out to the Coast. Did a little work along the way when I ran out of money, but I wasn't tempted to stay anywhere. Not even Los Angeles. Must've passed right through where Ray was at that time. Bunked for a while with some folks I met, but I took a train up the coast first chance I got, almost stayed in San Francisco.

They were listening to a whole different kind of music from what I was used to. Instead of Merle Haggard and Tammy Wynette, they were tripping to Jimi Hendrix and singing along with Aretha Franklin. The Rolling Stones, Santana, Led Zeppelin, Janis Joplin, The Doors, Steppenwolf and Buffalo Springfield almost drowned out my memory of Buck Owens, Johnny Cash, Glen Campbell, Loretta Lynn and Marty Robbins!

Eventually I took a ride with some hippies who had a bus and were heading to Oregon to start a farm commune, or so they said, when they were capable of saying anything. Cut loose from them outside of Eureka though. They sure weren't going anywhere in a hurry, and though they were nice enough folks, they stayed high all the time and I found I did not like being that kind of out of control. Got me thinking then, what kind of control I did want. In my life. By then the ranch was far behind, but I still felt like I had to get all the way up to Seattle before I made up my mind.

I was on a ride about halfway through Oregon, when all the traffic stopped, and I got out to see what had happened. It had just happened, I couldn't tell how, but there was a wreck, two of them, all over the road, and folks left lying around, some moaning, one of them crying. It was maybe the worst feeling I'd ever felt, not being able to do anything, for any of them. State troopers were pulling in, some of them shoving back the gawkers, like me. And they went right to work on first aid, doing what they could. And

I knew that's what I wanted to do. Nothing exact, just to be able to help when something bad like this happened.

When I got to Seattle, everyone was complaining about the economy, Boeing this and Boeing that. And there were no jobs, at least not for young cowpokes out of Texas. I did meet some folks though who put me up a while in exchange for chores, and they told me about the new community college and how I might start taking some courses to get into medicine. It sounded good to me. It sounded like nothing I had every been or thought about back in Estacado County. It sounded perfect.

There was a lot of hippie stuff going on then in Seattle too, but it just wasn't for me. I guess I had spent so long working hard everyday that it had become a habit. Maybe even a craving. I went looking for something to do outside of classes and was walking by a fire station when I was nearly run over by an aid truck pulling out, sirens screaming. I watched it swerve down the street, dodging traffic, and disappear around a corner. There were some guys standing around inside the station, and I just went right in and asked how I could do what those other guys were doing. Medics. They laughed at me, maybe at my accent, but when I didn't laugh with them and got that look on my face, they stopped, gave me some coffee and we got to talking.

I was just getting set to start some basic aid courses with them when I got my draft notice. All that time, I hadn't paid much mind to the war, never occurred to me to get a college deferment. It was all so far away, seemed like it just had nothing to do with me. I don't recall that I really minded having to go, except for interrupting my medical studies. I went over to the local Army office and told them I wanted to volunteer as a combat medic.

But if I thought that was all there was to it, I soon learned otherwise. My life changed again, and not for the better. The maverick was hog-tied, branded and sacked in olive drab. And yelled at worse than most of my brothers had ever managed.

Morning formation they called it. Every damn day. Reveille, wake up, personal hygiene, dress for the day and be standing tall in the Company area when the whistle blew. Roll call, then some routine inspection by the NCOs, a chance maybe to go on sick call, then the training schedule for the day was read out, and we got assigned our place in line for chow.

"Bird, Charles!"

"Present." Some others in line looked at me, still struck I guess by my drawl.

"Trainee? What's the matter with you? Fall out here young soldier!"

I stepped out of formation and walked over to stand in front of Sergeant Piña. I knew what he was after, or thought I did. He wanted a loud 'Yes Sergeant!' out of me. I just couldn't get the hang of that.

"Bird, what're you doing in This Man's Army?"

"Training," I told him, almost conversationally.

He stiffened, at my easy tone, I guess. "Training? I tell you when you are training. You do not know shit. What are you training for, Bird?"

"Basic now Sergeant, then Medic training at Fort Sam?"

Sergeant Piña moved even closer to me, nose to nose. "You in love with me Bird? You want to marry me?"

"No, I don't believe I do."

"Then why you tell me all this shit. I don't want to know anything about you. You know why? Because the Gooks are going to kill you, Bird. They gonna kill you and six of your friends, you know that? You know why?"

I knew he wanted a big-voiced 'No Sergeant' but what he got instead was just, "No I do not know."

"That's right," he kept yelling. "You do not know. You got no idea. Get back into formation! Unless you gonna fly away right now? I see you want to cry, Bird. Man." He added the last word under his breath in apparent disgust.

I turned to go back to my place in line. I guess I did want to cry, I couldn't help it. But I wasn't going to.

"Bird! You stop right there. You turn around and look me in the eye like you want to kill me."

I gave him the look. And I was pleased to see it register.

"That's right. Better!" And he turned then and began to strut up and down the line of us, talking to the others in line, rather than me. "I do not care if you live or die Trainee! But I am going to train you so you do not get everybody else killed!"

Then he turned back directly and his eyes cut into me like bullets. "As you were."

I returned to stand between the trainees I'd fallen in with that morning, Oates and Funderbirk, the one they called Tbird. I guess my face was pretty hot and sweat ran down my back even in the cold of that damp morning. I put my eyes straight ahead.

Then, almost as if Piña could read my thoughts, the old Sergeant barked again, "You think you gonna get special treatment here because you gonna be a medic? Save lives? You sick call dropout! That's the only way you get close to a medic Bird! You weak, that's why you don't want to fight! I can't wait to get you into the ring with me, and I tear off your arms, pussy!"

The wave of anger I felt then (the kind I've felt many times since) actually did leave me weak. I was wobbly from it. I don't believe I had ever been so mad in my life, and that's going some. Oh yes, I wanted to get into the ring with that asshole! Right then and there. Maybe I'd just forget all that stuff about saving lives, and kill this bastard first chance I got.

"Forget it man" Tbird said, under his breath. "He just shittin' in your helmet. Pick on you 'cause you don't yell back, 'cause you act like you been to college, want to make somethin' a yourself. He don't like the look in your eyes, you thinkin' you better than him."

"I don't think that. Well, I do now. But not before."

"Bullshit. You think you better than everybody here. I don't mind. You probably are. I like that what he call you. Birdman. You alright. You save my ass someday, Birdman?"

Birdman. Not the last time I would hear that, though it's been a long time since. Hadn't thought about it again til now.

I did save his ass. Later. I don't know how it got arranged that way. We all finished basic and I went off to Fort Sam for medic training, just like I had said, and I don't know where Tbird went for AIT. We didn't write. We didn't have much in common. I don't know when he was sent to 'Nam. Probably not more than a couple months after I went to Texas. Him sweating in the jungles while I was playing Dr. Kildare in an air-conditioned hospital wing by day and drinking beer and shots in a local dive by night. And when I was through, I also went to Vietnam. But I never thought about Tbird, or Oates, or any of the rest of them from basic. Not even Sergeant Piña.

I flew in like everybody does and eventually got motored out to a company dug in around Pleiku to replace the doc that was rotating out of the unit, going home. And then I forgot about everybody and everything. At least I tried to. I just wanted to get done, stay alive, and keep some of the guys that way too so they could go home, if not in one piece, at least with all the pieces they still had sewn together.

One day, I got sent over to a different platoon and I wasn't looking to find anybody I knew. I wasn't looking to make any friends. Mostly, a doc can't afford to make friends with people he's gonna have to cut and sew, kids whose organs he may get to see. Men whose lifeless corpses he's going to ignore while he looks for the living.

That platoon went out on patrol the same night I dropped my stuff on the empty bunk and I went with them.

It was all the same old shit. Night sounds oppressive. Unrelenting heat and humidity clinging to us all like a shredded filthy blanket. Vigilance dialed way up past the end of the range. Waiting for something to happen, knowing it almost certainly would not, at least not that night. Everything strung as tight as a cheap piano wire. We were mostly single file on an almost non-existent track. No speaking allowed at all, everything taped and strapped in. When somewhere up the line I heard a small pop and dropped like a stone to hug the damp earth, along with every other guy near me. The flash and sound of the explosion and the rip and tear of angry shrapnel bees over my head just a blip after the first sound. And in a heartbeat the screams. And the incoming fire.

Everybody returned fire immediately, in all directions, but we were badly exposed. The shredding vegetation providing no cover at all, just the dangerous illusion of relative safety. We heard orders from the NCOs to scatter and dig like motherfuckers. And to hold our fire for a vector to sight on. Empty magazines were pulled and replaced with the click-clack we knew too well. And I low-crawled in the direction of the moans and cries.

"Doc! Over here!" Someone called. I slithered over to some men where two had fallen, one of them way dead. The other was Funderbirk. His eyes were rolled up so only the whites were showing, and his teeth were chattering so hard I had to put a stick in his mouth and tell his buddy to hold it there so his teeth wouldn't break.

"Tbird, buddy." I said, close to his ear, rounds ripping just over my head, two men right beside us firing back at the incoming volley, semi-auto. "Tbird, it's me Birdman! Listen to me!" I hissed.

One of his pupils came into sight in the near darkness while I risked a little hooded light for a quick triage then snapped it quickly off. "You're going home buddy! This one's bad enough. We're gonna patch you up right now and get you outta here. Your mama gonna be glad to see you."

"Birdman?" he croaked in a quaver. "You alright."

I don't remember noticing when the shooting stopped. I gave Tbird some morphine and tied off the worst of his bleeding, had his buddy put compression on the wounds in his torso while I crawled along the line to check off the dead, and do what I could for the others, mostly instructions to buddies to apply pressure and keep telling them they would be ok. Some of the guys who were not hurt looked worse then the ones who were. I asked for them to be jostled and talked to, for now. Tbird was the most serious case, and I could not cross him off, even if that were possible for me. I hadn't thought about him once since basic, and I did not see any way we could have called each other friends. I didn't even know if he still had a mama. I only knew right then that if he was my own sister, I could not have loved him more, or been more willing to be in his place and he in mine.

I worked on him until almost dawn, taking breaks to attend to the other less seriously wounded and to refresh my instructions and dispense pain meds and supplies to the orderlies I had pressed into service for their friends. Tbird was slipping away. More from shock it seemed to me than blood loss. But then I had no way to estimate the degree of possible internal bleeding. I had one leg splinted and wrapped from a clean shrapnel break of the shin. And had already sutured several deep wounds to one arm and shoulder and part of his cheek. There was no suction in the chest wound, and no organs exposed in the abdomen. Just your basic shot to pieces mess.

"Tbird! Listen to me man! You are going to make it! You are going to walk away from this! You are going home, right now!" I watched for signs he could hear me, was processing, would rally. Nothing. His pulse and breathing were weak but regular. One eyelid fluttered a bit then and his lips parted and he said something I could not hear. I leaned down, stroked his good cheek and hissed into his ear, "Talk to me Tbird."

He shuddered and drew a breath that I could see hurt him to take and whispered, "Birds gotta fly together ... take me home Birdman." And though I could see by the grimace that smiling hurt too, he did it anyway. Just a little bit. The sound of the Hueys coming in to the LZ that the grunts had improvised was lost to him as he calmly passed out.

The lead gunship hosed the perimeter for us with the gattling, and we strapped up and ran with our dead and wounded for the dust off.

● ● ●

The crunch of wheels on pavement, deceleration and sounds of landing shake me out of this ... reverie.

I unfold myself painfully from the pencil thin body of the regional jet that has just arrived at San Luis Obispo. The southern sky like nothing I have felt since maybe Texas, or Southeast Asia. No humidity though, just that clear liquid light spilling down and around me, through me. Strangely energizing me. California.

I had called ahead, got instructions from the prison authorities, wrote ahead to Clayton Ray telling him I was just a writer and asking if I could come for a visit. Though I knew better. But she, Tuyet (I say her name to myself, and get that small mental jolt again that is like putting a piece of foil in my mouth), had charged me on no account to reveal any hint of her relationship to Ray, or of my relationship to him through her.

That last part will be easy. Because I feel no relationship at all. I know almost nothing about him, his life. Beyond the clippings she left with my editor, and maybe a bit more research on him I have already started. But what is that? In a man's life, I mean. His whole life. Or my whole life, for that matter. Separate paths.

The clippings tell a story that must have been common in those days, in that war, that country. A black man is singled out for punishment, never mind the facts. A trouble-maker, likely, but not a quality unique to his race. I knew many of them. Black, Hispanic, and many, many White. But few of them felt the combined wrath of the US Military like that certain breed of dark-skinned charismatics, who knew what was what and were fearless in speaking out about it.

You know the boy in the story of the Emperor's New Clothes? The one who declared for all to hear that the emperor wasn't wearing any clothes at all? Well, imagine that boy an angry, unapologetic black man telling everyone in a Jim

Crow Mississippi hamlet in the 1950's that the White Man was a hateful, lying murderer and was never under any circumstances to be trusted or obeyed. Now imagine the reaction of those citizens, but put them all in uniform and give everyone all the guns and ammunition and explosives they can carry. And put them in what amounts to a free fire zone with license to shoot anything and everyone on sight?

That's the atmosphere Clayton Ray chose for his platform to speak out. And it appears he spoke plenty. Even made veiled threats on the lives of officers (but no more than most of us did, and like most of us, I suppose, without any intention of ever carrying out any such thing.)

And when a grenade exploded in camp, killing two of the three officer occupants of a guest hooch, a hooch that was supposed to hold the company commander? Who do you think got accused, and practically lynched? Clayton Ray.

It remains a wonder that he wasn't killed right there. Or later convicted of the murders, even though his legal team had succeeded wildly in getting the trial transferred stateside to Fort Ord in California. It transpired miraculously that the all white, all officer jury simply could not piece together enough of the skimpy bits of so-called evidence to sustain a verdict of guilty. The hasty frame the Army had hung together as an afterthought had simply fallen apart.

The shrill whoops of a metal detector I just set off shove my head down into my shoulders, explode my brain and stop me in my tracks, paralyzed between wanting to run, and wanting to dive for cover. An icy sweat beading under my eyes and on my upper lip, droplets already coursing down my spine. Everyone is frozen, shocked at my reaction, and I quickly realize what has happened and tell them, "Sorry. It's the metal fragments. I forgot to tell you."

I am deep in the bowels of confinement now and a good natured correction officer (they don't like to be called guards anymore) tells me not to worry and motions me aside with his extended detector wand to a spot marked on the floor. "It happens. You serve?"

"Yes, I did."

"Where? You're too old for the Gulf."

"A long time ago, another place."

"Oh. Vietnam."

I don't reply and he wands me all over, his instrument chirping and squeaking over every foot of my body. As he has me turn out my pockets to be sure, he mutters "Jesus. What've you got in there?"

"Nobody's ever told me for sure. Probably a little of everything. Do I need to strip? I don't want to talk about it, alright?"

He looks over at the man in charge of the detail who shakes his head. "Nope. Guess not. All clear here." This last he calls out in ritual formula to the woman on the gate, who buzzes it open and motions for me to walk through.

I am uneasy here, behind walls, surrounded by fences and locked gates. Immersed now in a population of men for whom this has become their whole life. Regulated, controlled. Immutable. I feel as if my lungs have filled with a slurry of wet concrete, now setting up, soon to be rigid. Then no more breathing. My shoes get heavy and my walk seems more and more uphill, though I can plainly see that the floor is level. I feel three sizes smaller, and shrinking.

The institutional smells too, though nowhere near what popular fiction calls to mind, are pervasive, oppressive, driving out even the memory of sun-washed open spaces, of rain cleansed air. I tremble with ghostly memories ... .

But the officers I have so far encountered, men and women, have been nothing but genial, even cordial to me. I tell myself to relax.

I am shown by my escort into a small room furnished only with metal table and three chairs, the walls an off gray, the floor polished linoleum, smelling of fresh wax and the loss of centuries. The door closes behind him as he leaves me in the room. Alone. I look around warily. There's an aerial photo of the Camp, what some of the inmates call this place, Camp Snoopy. The photo is high on a wall adjacent another wall with a high narrow window, through which I can see only the unrelenting blue of the unreachable California autumn sky.

The door opens, and a tall black man in prison blues is escorted in by a different officer. He stops just inside the doorway, his neck permanently sunken down in a prisoner's slouch, shoulders forward as if to keep his hands always in front of him where he could keep track of them, his eyes on me sitting in one of the chairs. He stands like that, waiting. His regard is not unkind, certainly not hostile. But neither is it interested, beyond what ordinary care a prison environment requires when meeting a new quantity. Me. With my own hands folded in my lap in front of me.

I start to stand, to extend a hand in greeting. He steps forward rapidly then, around me, ignoring my hand, his eyes on some item at a distance far greater than the walls of this room, or even what could be seen through the window.

"Mind your manners, Ray." The officer states flatly. "Let me know when you are finished," he says to me and leaves, pulling the windowed door closed behind him.

"Mr. Ray, thank you for agreeing to see me." I've dropped my hand to my side and stand slightly stooped myself, embarrassed after all this. In front of a man of mystery, history even, to whom it appears I am now related.

At my greeting, he stops under the window, with his long back to it, his gaze once more on me.

"Would you like to sit down?" I move my hand clumsily to indicate one of the chairs. He makes no indication he has seen or heard me. "I was hoping we could talk ... that is, if you still want to?" I feel like a kid again, in the Principal's office.

"About what?" he says to me in an accent vaguely familiar to my Texas-born ears.

I stutter out, "About ... whatever you like. I mean, I came to meet you, speak with you. It seemed right. And I was hoping you would ... tell me your side of things?"

He moves slowly but with no sign of injury or pain over to the chair I've indicated and sinks slowly down onto it, keeping his watchful eyes easily on my face. "Don't know. I said alright to your coming down here. I was curious. Don't get many white visitors." His accent has gone even deeper South and he says 'white' just like you'd refer to something you couldn't clean off your shoe.

Then, with no southern notes at all, and only a trace of ebonics, "Suppose you start. You tell me why you are here. What you want from me."

6

Iraq. Al Anbar Province.
_/_/2007. The Present.

There has been no fighting for a week. I think I may be starting to lose it. And I am definitely starting to wonder about Blake and Rivers.

We are not Boy Scouts over here. At least I'm not. And some of us like it better over here than others. Everybody gets scared when we hear a blast, or the thwy-ippp of a near-miss supersonic round. Everybody's balls drop to the ground at the rattle of automatic fire. It's a natural reaction, a lifesaver sometimes.

But some of us get a tiny little wrinkle in a corner of the mouth, or the eye, an unnatural smoothing out of just a little bit of the forehead. And you can hear a little hum from inside of them – not a song hum, but a kind of revving-up, a rising whine, like a big electric motor, or a jet engine. They are in the zone, they are ready to do with a kind of feral pleasure, what the rest of us only do out of desperation.

That's Blake and Rivers. And that's not the part to wonder about. It was pretty clear to most of us that they were the killers in our unit. And while there is no identifying with them, it is easy enough to go with a little admiration of their calm, their cool efficiency in a gunfight, especially if it is helping to save your ass. I just hate what they stand for, otherwise.

I am crouched near our bivouac and looking up into the sun, even though I shouldn't be. If the sun is where everything started, shouldn't there be some answers coming from that direction? The air above the sand is shimmering, like water on a cool day in a faint breeze. I can almost feel the ripples on my skin ... water ... I feel like I am slowly sinking ... . Everything is impossibly white. My head aches like it is being squeezed. Then it all goes dark for a second, and my heart actually does sink ...

And there right in front of me *is* a stream. I think it is. And I think I know this water, its surface oily smooth and littered with bits of jungle torn by winds or blown from shrapnel in the next sector's war. Dark, too. Impossible to see beneath, to see what might be swimming around in it, what might be sunk in it. What might be waiting in it.

Another stream to cross I hear myself think, and I think of my socks still wet from the last crossing. Sunk, is right, I say under my breath. I can see in my mind an image of us grunts just quietly on the hump in the sand today but it grows dim and fades. I have a real sense of loss.

Probably the same stream we've already crossed today and maybe three times yesterday, I think to myself. Myself? Did I cross those streams? In this jungle? Part of me thinks it looks like the same stream. Like a guy in a movie I saw, talking about being uncomfortable with his memory, says "I remember perfectly, remember it all happening – I just don't remember doing it." That's me, right now.

Now I am stepping into the water, soon up to my waist, the water so warm there is barely any sensation of wet. What I am feeling is that some personal hell has a new charge just waiting to be ignited by the spark of this crossing. The sense of threat is a bitter tightness in the back of my throat, though any picture of what might actually be looming is as vague as spider silk across the back of my neck.

"Hey Birdman, you wade that water like a virgin, can't tell how to get into the pussy," a guy calls from behind, laughing his silly high-pitch 'hee hee' laugh. I know him. Brasso, I think we call him.

"Fuck you Brasso. Everybody knows how to get into yours," I find myself returning at him, without much thought. The others laugh too. Good for them. Not much to laugh at out here.

I keep moving forward, cautiously, sliding my front foot, with my weight on the rear, probing for vines or trip wires, or holes, then lifting the foot, knee high to advance another step across the stream. I wonder for just a moment at how natural this all seems to me, like I do this all the time.

It's clear to me that it's my turn to point the stream, the others waiting, weapons to the shoulder, ready to lay down suppressing fire if the Gooks open up. I'm exposed, out in the middle of the water, not much help for that. I try to swallow what's clinging to the back of my mouth, raise my weapon to high port. An exercise in maintaining a rational calm in the midst of some hidden, not-yet-exploded attack, and for which my dry weapon may be my only asset. I taste bug repellant running down my nose with the sweat of the midday sun only dimly seen through the canopy far above. No trips, no drops, so far. Near the far bank, bamboo advancing in a line down the opposite slope, down into the water, like a curtain drawn across the next act.

I stop then in the shallows, near the bamboo covered bank, turn my shoulders to look back across at the guys, each strung along the far bank in whatever cover and crouch they can manage, waiting my signal for their turn to cross. None of them are much encouraged by my safe passage so far. The VC wouldn't open up on a single man if they thought they could bag the whole squad.

I probe carefully with my muzzle for crossed vines or wires strung in the bamboo, step up and into the thicket to test if I can get through, and when I think there is almost no chance that an ambush could be waiting for us, I curl my arm toward them and they start across the stream.

"Birdman, get your head out of your ass," the Gunny says to me, so close he could lick me. Startled, I rise a bit from my crouch alongside a dune with my weapon at port, and look around. No water. No jungle. No Brasso, or any of the other guys. My whole platoon here has stopped. And they are all looking at me. WTF. I see a couple swinging dicks are keeping back a laugh, but most are just looking at me like my head really *is* coming out of my ass. I stand all the way up, look out across the desert, see the heat dancing up in waves from the sand, feel the sun high. Feel, well, really lost. What was that? Water? Jungle? What just happened to me?

And the way I was talking, my thoughts? Who was I? I lower my rifle to carry in my left hand, and wipe my palm across my forehead and eyes. Plenty of sweat, but no fever. I look at the Gunny. He shakes his head at me and signals for the platoon to form up, and we get back on patrol.

7

CMC - San Luis Obispo
_/_/2007. The Present.

So. I can't leave the past alone, or it won't leave me alone, and now it looks like I have a future I can't get rid of either. Ray wants me to tell him why I am here, what I want. And it's that or leave, I think. I can't tell him his granddaughter sent me. I can't tell him that I come from his past. My past.

When they let me go from Madigan Army Hospital where they sent me to convalesce after a hundred surgeries and a thousand docs with experimental knives and staples, I was still having the dreams. Every night, sometimes all day. Little shadowed faces. Eyes with points of starlight and fire. At night. And in the blazing sun, the flies and the unspeakable stench of pointless death.

Always the eyes. Those eyes I never saw in life, but only guessed at, quailed in fear they had seen me, found me, were adjusting the angle of their rocket tubes or building a site picture on the side of my head even as I thought of them. They did not know me. They just wanted me dead. Or better yet, wounded. Wounded I would be taken away by others.

Over there, the eyes I could see were not in brown faces, but blackened. With smoke, with flame, with the smear of grease sticks. Or bloodied. Or worse. Angry eyes, pleading eyes, eyes staring at a distance too great to measure.

When they wheeled me out the door, I had some pills for the pain, a prescription for more. What seemed like a lot of money in my pocket, my civvy slacks pocket. I had the shirt on my back, a surplus field jacket and a pair of my old class A shoes. And a duffel, mostly empty, with everything else in the world I owned. And no place to go.

Not home. No way. Not even for Eileen, and she was the one I did care about. She hadn't written in all the time since I'd left or, if she did, they hadn't caught up with me by the time I got blown up. And nothing came for me in the hospital. Most likely she hadn't. I never did. What would I have said?

So, not back to Estacado County. Where then? Back up to Seattle? It wasn't far north of Madigan and wasn't that where I had headed, long ago? What had I been thinking. Nevermind. I didn't want to know. Anyway there'd be no one there who would bother me. That was for sure. As good a place to have my dreams as any. I stuck out my thumb.

The couple who picked me up only asked me where I was going. They left me alone. That was good of them. Maybe I looked scary, sort of, after I was in their back seat, hunched against the window, looking at nothing they could see, nothing they would want to see. I felt soiled, in their car, in their silence. I tried not to rub off on anything inside, and when we got to something that looked like city, I asked to be let out near a truck stop. They wished me luck, but they were not sorry to see me go. I made up my mind to take a bus from wherever I was, imagining the relief of anonymity in seats either empty, or partially filed with other shells like me. And no one even thinking of social intercourse.

Turned out this was the Tacoma I had heard vaguely about. It held no promise for me and maybe nothing would. I ordered a sandwich and coffee, ate a few bites and left to stand outside and smoke the last of the pack I had with me. And think.

Why Seattle? Why not just here. Maybe I wasn't ready then for what I became later. This place looked like bust to me, and I wanted prosperity, or at least commerce, surrounding me. I did not want it for myself, but I already hated other losers more than I hated myself, and I wanted that kind of warm water to float downstream in. I thought.

I had no idea where to find a bus, and it was late at night, so I stuck out my thumb again, and a truck pulled over. I hopped up and a dour looking driver said, "I know that look. And you might not believe it, but I know you too." There was no warmth in his tone, only familiarity. I must have looked skittish because he said, "Nah, don't worry. I don't want anything from you. You just relax and I'll get you where you're going. Heading for Seattle. I'll drop you at a place you can bunk for the night."

He merged with sparse traffic and I watched the lane lines, slumped in my seat.

"Sucks, don't it."

It wasn't a question, and I didn't respond. The only other thing he said, when he dropped me off, was "good luck, buddy." And I stood on a curb in front of a house on a hill with Hendrix' Purple Haze coming out through the walls.

Weeks went by. Months maybe. I had no sense of the weather or the season, barely knew the time of day, and not even that sometimes. I spent a lot of time asleep. With those dreams. When I couldn't stand them anymore, I would get up, drink a beer and get high if I could. No one spoke to me, though I was usually not alone. The others were too much like me and they knew better. They barely spoke to each other. Every once in a while I would notice a now more or less familiar face no longer showing up, and one or two new faces. But no socializing. Like we each had our time to serve in perdition and no point in messing around with it.

I never stopped thinking and dreaming, never even slowed down, but my body wasn't hurting as much, and I was losing the thoughts of maybe just getting so wasted I could sleep with no dreams and never wake up. I went down the block and out onto Broadway and got ice cream at a place where people would at least not try to spill their happiness onto me. Sometimes one or two of the fellas at the place I lived would tag silently along and I would treat them, but only if they kept their thanks to themselves. We'd walk back along quiet streets and be sure to say nothing at all as we ate our cones or dishes of sweet Americana. I couldn't think of anything else I might ever want. I did not waste energy wondering if this was all there would ever be, for me.

One night, I was walking back with one other kid, one skinnier even than me, and hair much longer than mine, when a car drove by with boys hanging out the windows.

"Hey Faggots! Get off the streets!" one yelled. And another threw something, hit my ice cream partner in the head and dropped him to the ground like a sack of fertilizer. Laughter, cackles and calls erupted from the car.

The kid was curled up on the ground holding his head and moaning so I guessed he wasn't hurt that bad. I don't remember what I said, as I stood there, but the car stopped and two or three of them got out, maybe others behind that I didn't see, and came toward me. The leader had his brow down and his hands fisted.

"Maggot, you are gonna get your ass kicked good," he said. The two immediately behind him looked like they were strolling to a spectacle they'd heard would be great fun. All grins and teeth.

When they'd first thrown the bottle, I felt a surge of fear and flinched out of the way, and loathed myself for caution and cowardice. There was an immediate boil of anger in my guts – a whole different kind of pain than what I had been feeling ever since I got killed. And a molten course of something that would harden up fast shot up from my loins, along my ribs and down the insides of my arms. By the time these joy riders got out of their car, I was moving toward them, without thinking about it, my head swiveling to measure terrain, angles, possible cover, and alert for ambush. By the time he'd finished telling me what was going to happen to my ass, I was accelerating in a crouch and springing for his middle with my head tucked safely to one side.

I drove into him like a tackling dummy, knocking all the air out of him, folding him like a loose bag of dirty laundry, and kept on driving him backwards right through and over his two grinning friends until I had his head slammed on the drip rail at the edge of the roof of his car. I turned my head quick to see his two buddies on the ground and stirring to stand and two more at the edge of the scene with their mouths open and their hands out wide in shock, and then I slammed his head twice more on the roof and dropped him when he went slack.

I drop kicked one of the former laughing boys right up the ass and was stepping over him to the other one now scrambling to get up, and with something more than just fear in his eyes, and I caught the peripheral motion of the other two racing to get back into their car. They gunned the motor and squealed the tires, leaving their friends alone. With me.

Number Two was backing away from me, both hands patting the air in a gesture of peace, of surrender. He started crying. "Please. Please. I'm sorry. I had no idea. I never meant anything. Please!" He was getting frantic. "Please don't hurt me!"

For some reason this made me even more angry. I felt the last of reason leaving me as I slammed down on his instep and caught his head in both hands and moved my thumbs for his eyes. He was screaming in terror, and suddenly he threw up all over me and started to choke on it. I spun him around and wacked him hard twice on the back and bent him over so he could recover, and backed off.

I could barely see anything by this time, my vision was filled with rage and with this kid's terror and humiliation. I felt sick myself and left him and turned to the kid that had been hit with the bottle. He was starting to rouse. I reached to pull him up, when I felt something let go inside me, and my legs collapsed. I went down to my knees. I felt shot, all over again, and sank to the distant wail of sirens and the pounding feet of escaping boys.

I was transferred from emergency to the VA hospital where they treated me for blood loss and the local police gave up on me as likely assailant since it now looked more like I was the victim. I got the details of this several days later, after I was in recovery from yet another surgery to repair the damage I had done to some of the many sutures in my guts.

One of the docs, who had served as a trauma surgeon on a hospital ship earlier in the war gave me some friendly advice. "Stay out of fights, Bud. Your hero days are over."

"For how long?" I asked without much interest in the answer.

"For how long? For ever. You were a corpsman, a medic, right? Do you know how little there is left inside you to sew anything else to?"

"Sure thing, Doc. Thanks." I said weakly and closed my eyes, not really having to pretend to fall asleep.

He stood over me a while, then moved off, saying under his breath as he left, "You did good, soldier."

In the dark, after he left, I could hear movement out beyond the wire, the never ceasing sounds of the Southeast Asian night. I saw a pair of eyes, liquid in the darkness, wise beyond years, suddenly blinded by the burst of a trip flare, and I ducked my own head and covered my neck with my hands as the first rounds came and exploded all around me.

You did good, soldier.

So.

I could not just tell Clayton Ray the biggest reason I had come to visit. And as for other reasons? I did not even know myself – not altogether. There was a pull here. A gravitation. Might as well ask myself how one tectonic plate crashes slowly into another. Might as well ask them why. I had my assignment. There was that. My chance to learn something. Something to get me started on speaking out? Saying my own piece? But now that I had read the clippings, now that I sat in front of the man himself, I was almost ashamed to pursue it, at least on its own terms. Make a story out of the life of this man sitting in front of me? And there was no doubt in my mind now that there was a story. A story of epic proportions, probably. But not for me to write. Not for me to write and then cheapen to sell papers. It made my head swim a little, and started to set my teeth on edge, sour my stomach.

I hear myself say, "Well, you were accused of some awful things, and they made it pretty hard for you. Then I gather you won the trial, and things were still pretty tough on you. And now this." I rotated both palms vaguely upwards, pumping them once. He gives no sign he's heard anything. "I thought you might want to tell it your own way?"

"You thought wrong. There was no trial," he says to me, energy rising in his tone, the universal dominant male signal to back off. "I did not 'win' anything." The emphasis on the last two words so stark I have to wonder if there's going to be a fight, and I have to hold myself to keep from looking at the door. "Everybody thought I did it. It was meant to be a whitewash."

I respond only with respectful attention, and his anger seems to cool.

He looks into my eyes for a while. Assessing? Daring? I can not tell. When there seems no help for it I say, "But you were acquitted."

Nothing changes at first. I wait. Then a small smile just at the corners of his mouth begins to grow. Slowly. When the smile reaches his eyes he adds, "You know, don't you, that in this country, a black man, even some white men, can be convicted of a crime, and it doesn't mean they did it." His cadence slows for emphasis on 'did it.' "Doesn't mean they did anything. Right?"

He looks for response, finds it in a blink of my eyes.

"Well then you must also know that being acquitted doesn't mean you *didn't* do it." He puts his hands on his knees and stands up, waves to his escort through the door window. He says, walking away, "As far as everybody is concerned I have been guilty of murder for the last 40 years."

He goes to the door and stands. Waiting for it to open. To let him out? Or back in.

But he turns then and says, "I don't care about that anymore."

He studies me a while.

"You wanna know about those days, ask my sister. Or my niece."

I'm not sure now what I want to know about. It's getting harder to imagine looking any further into all this. I don't want to. I think about what Tuyet would want. All I know for sure from her is not to tell Ray anything. No, that's not right. She also said she wants me to trace the path of Clayton Ray. But she didn't say I had to get it all from him. And somehow she wants us, both him and me, together. But I'm very fuzzy on that last part.

"Really?" I offer. "You wouldn't mind?"

"Mind? Yeah, I mind." Gives me the Look. "But you ain't gonna give up now, are you?"

"No. I guess not."

"Well then go and ask your questions – just do it somewhere else."

"What is her name? Their names."

"Emelda, my sister. And Louise, her daughter, my niece. She's probably a better one to see. Emelda doesn't talk to me anymore."

The door opens for him and he's gone.

8

San Luis Obispo
_/_/2007. The Present.

I drove my rental car back to the motel in San Luis where I had dropped my things on the way out to see Ray. My head was spinning, and it hurt too. I needed some time. Why? To get clear? 'Focused'? To consider if I even wanted to continue this business with Ray? I was out of my depth. I hadn't spent any time, for as long as I could remember – no time, considering anyone but myself.

Now I had this nuclear power source plugged into my life. Tuyet. So bright it hurt my eyes. And she wanted me here with Ray. So? Why should I care? Guilt? Fatherhood? Too late. And Ray? Bad tempered. A lifelong fuck-up, rotting in jail, where he belonged?

Where I belonged too, I thought. If he did, then we all did.

Why would I say that? Tuyet? But she did not have the power to bind me to Ray. Did she? Common grandchild? What did that amount to? Nothing to me. Nothing as far as Ray was concerned. What, then? He hadn't said 20 words to me. He obviously didn't like me, was even hostile to me. Thought I was an idiot. And white. Well, he was probably right about the idiot part. He'd had enough trouble in his life, why should he let me stir up more for him. I even liked him.

There. I threw myself down on the bed. I liked him. And for no reason that I could see. Certainly not Tuyet as our common offspring, whatever I was feeling about her – and the votes were not in on that.

My head was hurting and I was too tired to resist taking meds. I dug around in my bag, swallowed a pill dry and laid back down. After a while my eyelids closed and faces swam behind them. Ray. Tuyet. A little boy on a bench … .

Eileen.

*… out of a murky night,
tracers arcing across the sky, a
pervasive low whine of electrics
under everything, and a coppery
taste in my mouth, there are voices …*

*"No, she's not dead.
Astonishing. All her vital signs are
strong, and if anything her brain
function charts are all normal."*

"But she's on life support."

*"Yes. But that's because of the
trauma. I don't know, I can't explain
it. If we can get permission, I think
she is a candidate for neuro-
reconstructive surgery."*

*"You're kidding. You're not
kidding? That's Star Trek stuff,
speculations in the journals."*

"I know, and way out of my league."

"But?"

"There's a guy."

"There's a guy. Why am I not surprised."

From a safe and remote distance, I watch as plastic skull plates are made, perfectly measured to replace my entire skull. My brain sections placed one at a time in the plate sections, on dural tissue cloned from my own ruined dura, with the care of plutonium segments fitted into a hydrogen bomb. And then all bolted together, tentatively, and drawn closer and closer as the swelling subsides.

When the swelling goes down enough, consciousness returns, my consciousness. Along with pain. I am no longer watching. This is me, again. I am alive, I think. I can think, and reason, after a fashion. Not dead.

And the pain is just a thing to manage.

When I wake in the dark, I know it is all a dream. Except for the pain. That's real, and drives me stumbling from bed, looking for something to take. I find a light switch, look at the clock. Almost 4 a.m. While I rummage in my bag half blind looking for the serious medicine, I realize that the 'me' in the dream is a woman. I stop with a vial in my hand, the label incomprehensible as my vision arches out over the continent into the deserts of West Texas. Eileen.

I am dreaming about my sister. I am dreaming I am my sister. And I've been fatally shot, but I am not dead, and my head … . My head is now made of plastic plates held together with space-age hardware. The hand that is not holding the vial, my hand, reaches up to the crown of my head, expecting to find plastic seams … perhaps coming loose?

Eileen. Of course. I am not her. There's nothing wrong with my head. Except what's inside that I use for thinking. And I have to get to her. I know with sudden clarity.

I don't believe in this kind of thing and neither does she, last I heard. But this is urgent.

I notice I have a vial of some kind of meds in my hand. I have no idea why. I drop it in my bag with others like it, go looking for my wallet, think about taking a cab to the airport. Remember the car, find the keys and go.

On the way to my first lay over in San Francisco, I nap in starts and fits. The flight attendant is very kind to me, her eyes almost loving, if I am not imagining. Her name tag says Kerry. She brings me coffee that I did not ask for, but it smells good. Oddly, she asks me if there is something troubling me and leans on an empty seat back across the aisle with her ankles crossed to wait for my answer.

"No," I say automatically, politely. "Yes." I suddenly confess, then recant, "I mean, no, there's nothing special. ... I'm ... just ..."

"Worried," she finishes for me, but frames her face in a question, in case I want to disagree and supply something different.

"Yes. No." I cannot stop this equivocation.

"I see," she says, gently takes the coffee out of my hands, leaves and returns in a minute holding out a real glass with what looks like an ounce of bourbon in it. I take it from her. It is. "Tell me about it," she says simply, assuming her lean again.

"I had a dream last night, a bad dream. Very bad," I find myself saying, wondering only a little at my apparent willingness to talk to this stranger. Her face shows concern, and a gentle question. "When I woke up, it was like a premonition. If that's what they are like. I don't have them, I don't believe in them."

She gives me one slow nod.

"About my sister." I can't help thinking this woman will want no part of this.

Her head assumes a very slight angle of heightened attention.

With an abandon that surprises me, I plunge on. "Eileen is my only little sister. Out of eleven kids, I was nearly the youngest. Eileen was last. I cannot remember when we last talked. I think I have lost her."

That stops me. In a way, I have really lost her. I don't think she knows where I am. Or who I am, now. A great bubble swelling in my chest is threatening to burst, as I sit immobile in this flying coffin. It will burst, I want it to burst. I almost do.

And when it does, I will sob and this kind and attractive woman will look away, and tears will run down into my mouth and I will die. And it will be all over.

"Oh dear," says my listener, leaning slightly more toward me.

I taste salt on my lips, feel now the twin streaks of moisture already drying on my cheeks. I am crying. She is not looking away.

"Wait just a second," she says holding up one finger for the number of seconds I am to wait. She is back in just about that second with a warm cloth which she puts in my hand, raises my fingers to my own cheek. It is a vast and surprising comfort. She waits.

"Thank you."

"Of course." She waits then takes the cloth, now cooling, from my extended fingers. "I just know everything will be alright. You never have to prove your worth to the people who matter most to you." She smiles. "I do believe in premonitions, my own anyway. I have them all the time. You will find your sister. I know she does not want to lose you."

She takes the glass from my hand and turns to leave.

"Thank you," I hear myself say. And there's something in my voice. Something alive?

She smiles.

At San Francisco, before I boarded the plane to Denver, I debated whether to try and get in touch with Eileen ahead of time. But in truth, I had no idea how to do that. I had no memory of phone numbers at the ranch, and no great sense even of whether there still was a ranch, with or without Eileen. Without Eileen, there would almost certainly not still be a ranch. So, I figured I'd just rent a car and drive the near 100 miles from the airport in Odessa and confront whatever reality I found when I got there.

On the flight to Denver, the flight attendants seemed the usual helpful but impersonal folks I guess you always have. No one named Kerry, no one inquiring after me, or my thoughts, at least not beyond what I might want to eat or drink. I had nothing to read, and I found I did not want to think about Tuyet or Ray, or my strange visit, if that's what it was, to the desert. I thought about premonition.

Premonition in my life. I told Kerry I didn't believe in it. But I could see there had been many, many events in my life that were, even in some small way, foreshadowed by thoughts or visions of mine, or words that seemed spoken aloud in my head.

And even without any consideration of such foreshadowing, what about all the times in advance of some deadly action when I had just known we were going to get our asses handed to us? And what about that trip of mine to the desert? What about now, with Eileen?

I must have drifted off, and woke with my ears popping on the descent to the high plains. I had another long layover ahead of me, so I was in no rush to get off the plane. I would use the time in Denver to have a car ready for me in Odessa. I sat there as it emptied out, and noticed that I had not much experienced the claustrophobia that sometimes took hold of me on such flights. Maybe that was a good sign.

It's late when we drop down through cloud cover and land at Odessa. I go straight to the rental and start my drive to Babylon and the ranch, a long drive by Puget Sound standards, just a quick hop here in West Texas. It's after 8 and nearly dark when I start and it'll be later still when I get to the ranch. The hands will all be bunked down, but Eileen, if she's there, will still be up I am betting.

I can see myself on an aerial map of my route tonight, my car a speeding bullet to the heart of Babylon. And over that map I have superimposed a 2500 BC clay tablet map of Sippar in Iraq just north of ancient Babylon, one of Jerry Brotton's maps from his *History of the World in 12 Maps*. I like the comparison. The road to Babylon, then and now. Two plates now distant, once close. Then and now.

At a time when all the continents of the world had come together, when life, at least in the Sea, was as abundant as it had yet ever been, it was all wiped out. Or nearly all of it. The Permian extinction. And a hundred million years would go by before life's hold on the world, on the planet, would once again be so strong. And by that time, much of the old Permian sea bed had been shoved deep under the plates of the continents they collided with. Then and now.

Somewhere in that book of his, Brotton makes the point that "humans want to impose order and structure onto limitless space and time." As I drive through time and space at speeds exceeding 100 mph, it seems to me right now that I am doing something of the kind. Have been, too. Imposing limits. Maybe it is time for my own Permian extinction. And beyond that, for a long denied grip on my world, a strong grip. Something new for me.

I take the Interstate straight across since there will soon be nothing to see, I note with more disappointment than I would have guessed. Hadn't I seen all of this already? Enough for a lifetime? Virtual desert in some places, endless miles of grass, mountains in the distance. The Llano Estacado. I can still see all of that, in my head, even in the dark. With my eyes closed. Maybe that isn't what I ran away from. For there is some thrill here, I have to admit to myself. Along with a sense of return, and of memory.

In Texas, the town of Babylon was never large or important by any standards, even during the boom in the late 20s with the coming of oil to Estacado County. Oil brought hundreds of people to Babylon, scrambling over one another, living in tents or crude houses that used old derrick timbers as beams. But the mercurial nature of oil money and the western custom of boom towns also brought bootlegging, gambling, prostitution and other crimes to Estacado County and to Babylon in particular, with the city government believed to be in on the take. Dad told a story how one bad bunch ambushed and injured some of his ranch hands so he rode to town at the head of a posse and strung up two of the ring leaders on the spot right there in the town square. Dad never said, but it was well known around town that he was pronounced Sheriff then and there, an office he held for the rest of his life.

The railroad soon came in and linked Babylon and Estacado County to parts east and also to New Mexico. Dad met and married Helen Vieux from

Santa Fe, and settled down to build his ranch, maintain the law, and raise a family. In an uncharacteristic fit of optimism, my always well-grounded Mom insisted they rename the ranch Birdland. But three years passed and Mom did not conceive. That's when they adopted a baby and named him Steven, with the idea that they would never tell him he was adopted, I guess, not realizing the flood of mostly sons that was coming.

They'd wanted a big family, and I guess they loved each other. Besides, ranch life demanded a big strong family. After they brought in Steve, somehow the dam broke so to speak and nine kids got hatched. Steve always thought he was the first and oldest son, and acted like it. Except the part about honor your father, for he and Dad fought like wild animals.

When Steve got older, and bigger, even Dad walked around with bruises and cuts from their arguments. Mom never approved of their fighting, tried with everything she had to get them to stop. I think it made her grow apart from Dad, with every new cowboy at the table. Maybe it was even part of her downhill slide, though everyone assumed she was just worn out with taking care of eleven other people, giving birth to nine of them and, counting Steve, raising ten kids (this was before Eileen of course).

Anyway, when Mom got sick all the fight went out of Dad, and Steve started taking the old man's part. In fact, he just naturally took over the ranch, and everything about it. Sick with grief and with time on his hands for the first time in his life, Dad took up with a much younger woman he met in town, and one year after we buried my Mom, he and Vera were married.

Dad's own health didn't last too much longer after that. Vera had energy enough for both of them it seemed, especially since she didn't have much to do with our raising. Steve took over that too.

Some of the older boys were even wondering what else Steve was taking over. Everything, I guess. Who knows. Did Mom tell him that he was not actually related to the rest of us? Maybe out of some great need to clear her own conscience before she passed away? She's gone, so we'll never know. We could all tell though that he became very close to Vera, and the timing was close.

I mean, Dad died – Eileen was born after. Close enough after, it seemed, so on the surface she was Dad's last hurrah. Steve did treat her more like a daughter than a younger sister, though he had also been that way about all the younger kids, pretty much. Anyway, after Eileen was born, Steve was never the same around Vera again, and she kind of withdrew, into herself, and was never again close to any of us, except Eileen.

But I think all the older kids knew, or thought they knew. And they made both of the women pay for it. No one ever dared say a word about any of it to Steve.

Just south of Barstow, I take the service road across the Pecos, then south on the dirt track into the Chihuahuan desert country to Birdland, the family ranch.

It's moonless dark when my lights illuminate first the working fences of the corrals, and then the sprawling facade of the main house. There are a few lights still on in the cottages. Only the kitchen light in the big house. I stop, turn off the lights and the engine, and sit. Old demons stir in my blood and dance to the ticking of cooling metal. The porch light comes on, and a figure appears in the doorway behind the screen door. Then she steps out onto the porch and into the light, auburn hair pulled back tight from her face. My heart trills on a single long note, then sinks into my boots. I stay in the car with the door closed, not daring to move.

Neither does she, for long minutes, like she is listening to music, a very old, very sad Patsy Cline song. That nobody sings anymore. She lets the screen swat closed behind her and steps off the porch, slowly at first, then with gathering intent, and runs out to the interloper in the car. I open my door as she comes up, and she stops.

She looks ... good. Nothing wrong with her. I start to say "Eileen," but she cuts me off with her own quiet declaration, "Artemis." I step out and in two big strides catch her in my arms and swing her off the ground and around in a circle. Like when she was six.

With two pieces of pie gone, and several cups of Eileen's cowboy coffee providing buzz, I've finished telling her about my dream or vision in the motel in San Luis Obispo, asking her, searching her face, her eyes, to see if she is alright. She looks at me uncomprehending, as if I had asked her if she is considering a sex change. I love her! I would hug her now, again, if the table weren't covering my legs, and my leap wouldn't throw all the coffee and pie equipment into her lap. She might like it, at that.

No, I just smile like a big dumb brother, relief and gratitude coming out of my pores. I tell her why I was in San Luis, about meeting the young Tuyet. About what I learned about my own past in Vietnam, about Tuyet's grandmother. At this, she is not uncomprehending, she is stunned. But only for seconds. Something else dawns in her face, her eyes sparkle and she does leap up – only her agility saving me from getting coffee and pie dishes in my own lap. She is around the table and over me in my chair, her thin wiry arms around my shoulders, crying into my neck sobbing, "Artemis, Artemis …". I raise up one arm around her neck.

When she comes away, hands still steadying my shoulders, she looks angelic, radiant. "I am so happy for you. Sorry, too. About your girl. All those years ago."

That had not occurred to me. To be sorry, about her. For her. The sudden in-rush of it, coming as it did from my dear Eileen, is a small depth charge in my heart. The first throb almost breaks it in two. And then it stops beating for what seems like the rest of my life. I had buried that. Burned it down and buried it, like she said, all those years ago, and never looked back. I could not now even recall her face, except what came down in the face of my granddaughter. The sing-song of the club music, the smell of beer and sex rising in my senses to blur the edges of the kitchen, dull the sheen of the tears on Eileen's face. What a … what a son of a … what a rotten fucker I had been. Not in getting blown up, I added, my interior landscape now a courtroom of sorts, complete with defense counsel. No, that had not been my fault. But in running away, inside myself. Fleeing ... from what? From my love for this beautiful ... ? My throat swells, a great lump of broken metal, scorched earth, dried blood that I'll never be able to swallow. My face hot, hotter than ever, and with chill streams running down it, salt past the corner of my open mouth, my fingers clenched to fists, pounding, pounding ... pounding.

"Arty stop! Stop!" I hear her crying, feel her shaking me. Then pinning my arms, trying to, my fists starting to flail. "Charles Artemis Bird! God damn you, stop!"

I stop. I notice one fist poised to strike at the forces, the person, restraining me. It all goes out of me. My self loathing, my long denied sorrow, my violence. Only tears left. And sobs. Great racking sobs as Eileen throws herself onto my lap and holds me tightly. "I'm sorry," I bawl. "I am so sorry, so sorry. So ..." My tear soaked vision barely adequate to note the wreckage of the kitchen table, the fragments of china scattered everywhere.

I ran down. I got so tired I could barely sit up on my chair. Somewhere in there, Eileen had gotten up, started clearing up the mess. All the while talking softly to me, sure, it seemed likely, that I wouldn't understand much of what she was prattling. Just keeping company, she was. Maybe a few words about Steve. Where was Steve? What had become of him? Then nothing.

I woke up with the clear, early desert sun slanting in over my covers, in a bed I did not recall laying down in. In a room I did not know.

There is a soft knock at the only partially closed door. "Are you decent?" she warns, coming on through, with a tray in her hands. She stops at the foot of the bed, surveying, assessing, like she would a new foal at its first wobbly attempts at standing.

"Coffee?" she asks, walking over to the dresser under the window and setting down the tray. Carrying a cup and saucer over to me without waiting for any answer and setting it within spilling distance of my right elbow.

The smell is – exquisite. I sit myself up, shove the pillow behind my back.

"It's French," she tells my questing nostrils. "I like it when I want something fancy. The special china too. Remember Mom's set she ordered from Paris? Before I was born," she adds.

She means my mom, the one we both always called Mom, not Vera, her own mother. I always think it's a loving deference to me, because she really did adore Vera.

"I'm just glad I didn't have this set out last night, when you went all raging bull on us!" she laughs. And it's perfect. There isn't going to be any heavy discussion about my breakdown. That would be up to me, or not. This sister of mine is a wonder. I think, what is there she might not be capable of? The quick answer is, not much.

"Try it," she motions with her chin at the coffee by my side, then steps over and picks up her own cup and saucer, turns and sips, looking over the cup rim at me, with what looks like some mischief in her eyes.

I do. It is almost as good as it smells. I didn't want to offer her any comment based on a comparison between any French coffee and almost any kind of Seattle coffee. This is special for Eileen, so it is special for me. I make appreciative sounds.

"There's pancake batter by the griddle, and when you feel like it, we can go out and have eggs and bacon with them. On the dining room table." She cracks a tooth-filled grin.

I have to laugh, and I'm surprised at how good that feels. The laugh. Even just a bit. "Ok," I allow, "but all that might be too much for me. I don't have the appetite you remember!" I smile at her.

"Oh, you will, Brother. Wait till I set you riding fence!" She laughs some more.

And it crosses my mind to just let everything go and do that. Ride fence. Get down to ranching here with her. Maybe like I never left. So it occurs to me that I am actually having a thought about living here, again. And there is no lurch in my stomach, no revulsion at the thought. It could be … natural.

But then, I know I am not going to do that. I know, as I had not known when I left Ray at Camp Snoopy, that I will be going back. That I really am committed to Tuyet's mission. Somehow now, strangely, my mission. And I have a feeling it'll work out. All that takes only a second.

"Ha ha, yep – you would love that Little Sister, but you know I can't."

"Yes, I do know that. I just wasn't sure you knew it." Her face serious now, but still warmed by her smile.

We look at each other. My face feels warm too, but I do not know what it looks like. Except maybe by reflection in her own face.

She moves over, cup in two fingers, saucer in the other hand, and sits with me on the edge of the bed. "You know, I know what that dream of yours was about." She sips. And waits.

"You do?"

"Uh huh. It was your brain in pieces, waiting to be put back together. Those plastic plates are yours. And it looked like me because you needed to come back here and find me, so you could start finding yourself." She puts her cup in her saucer and looks almost smug.

"Ha," I say, though I do not find it funny.

"Yep. Like you started last night." She takes a quick sip, stands up and puts the empty cup and bottom back on the tray. "I'll be in the kitchen Artemis, when you feel like getting up and getting to work," she quips, chin raised. Then practically flounces out of the room.

We have breakfast together, as if she has nothing else to do all day, as if there were no ranch to run. I ask about Steve.

"It's been years, and no word." She looks wistful.

"Do you miss him?"

"Oh. Yeah," she says, "but not in that way." She changes the subject pointedly. "The boy? Tuyet's father? Does anyone know anything about him?"

"If they do, I don't know about it," I tell her, a quick flash picture of the boy on the bench crossing my mind, me almost dismissing it immediately, then relenting and letting it linger. Just a bit longer.

"And Clayton. In prison. That's awful."

I almost feel bad now because that thought has not occurred to me. It is awful. My chin down just that bit, I keep my thoughts to myself.

"Well, I am sure you will know what to do. And I will love you while you are doing it, Artemis." She reaches to put a hand on my arm. I slide my chair a bit and bend to kiss her on the cheek. She smiles, puts her palm to her face where my lips touched. "I love you," she says with a mixture of the fierce and the soft in her face that she holds for a long moment. "Now git on yore horse and ride."

• • •

It is a mystery - how we give our hearts before we give our thoughts, before we give our trust. How we give our hearts to folks before we know them well at all? What is that? What calls to our hearts? In what language? What deep pool covers the linkage that is formed – between one heart and another, on information imperceptible to thought, unquantifiable in analysis?

9

CMC - San Luis Obispo
_/_/2007. The Present.

I am heading back to San Luis, and Clayton Ray. I don't need to question why. I believe him when he tells me that he won't discuss his past. So I plan to visit him again and tell him some of mine.

All the officers seem to know me now, and the entry formalities go quickly. Then I wait in the same bleak room as before for Ray to join me.

He comes in the same as before, giving no indication he has seen me before, goes to stand by the high window looking at the sky. "You a slow learner, Mr. Bird? Or are you back to piss me off?" he says conversationally with his back to me.

"Neither," I correct him. "I came back to tell you something, not to ask."

"Ah," he says to the window ledge above him. "And what do I need to be told? Is there anything you think I haven't heard before?"

"Nothing like that," I say sitting down at the table, scraping the chair a little, the sound drawing first his shoulder, then his head around. "I came to tell you something about me."

He turns the rest of the way around to face me. "Now that will be very special. And I thought I was going to have to rearrange my lingerie collection this evening."

I try to ignore the sarcasm. "I know you have no reason to want to know anything about me, or maybe anyone else." I hold his eyes with mine. "But, aside from that lingerie, what else have you got going on in here?" I extend a hand at the other seat, meant as an invitation.

He looks at my hand as if there should be something on it, moves slowly to the other chair, pulls it out. "You really know how to sell a guy." He sits down.

"To begin with, I grew up in West Texas. And I was there, you know. Vietnam. Same time as you."

"And?"

"Just sayin'. That didn't go well for me either. Spent a lot of years messed up. Locked up."

He looks at me.

"They said I wasn't right in my head."

"Looks like they got that right. And you're telling me this why?" Not unfriendly now.

"Because I want to tell you something else. And you could think I'm crazy with this too."

"Tell me."

"I got hit by a car recently. You might think this is because I hit my head. It might be. But I don't think so."

He raises one brow.

"While I was out, or whatever, I woke up in the sand. With guys in uniform. And there was shooting. It was Iraq. I mean Iraq now, I think. I was there, it was incredibly real, more real to me than even this is. Than you are. But I was someone else. I was – it was like I was inside this other guy. A young guy. A Marine. Not possession or any junk like that. More like, along for the ride. I can't say it very well. I can hardly think of anything else sometimes. Anyway, I was there. I know it." I just look at him a long time.

"That it?"

"Yeah. That's it."

There's more I could tell him. About my family. Me the youngest boy of the bunch. My oldest brother Steve and my Dad always at odds. I look to see if anything is registering with him. Any kind of sign or tell.

He is not pretending to ignore me. Not looking at his fingers, the ceiling. That kind of thing. His eyes are open and watching me. His breathing relaxed.

I go on. "My whole family lived on a ranch, our ranch. Most of us in the big sprawling house my Dad started and Steve and the others continued with him. All the unmarried family each had their own room in the house, except my youngest sister and her mom Vera, and they had to share one. It was one of the earliest major fights I can remember, when I was old enough finally to get my own room, only because my next oldest brother moved out into his own room that the older brothers had just finished adding on to the house. I had only just started school and I thought my little sister should also have her own room and not have to sleep with her mom. So I said so, and of course, got shouted down. Bib, my 13 year-old brother actually said she would never deserve her own room, nor Vera either, because they weren't really family." Again I pause, trying to take a measure on this stolid black figure. It's starting to feel wrong, or at least awkward. I've never shared this story with anyone. But I go on.

"I practically knocked over the table I was sitting at, spilling the milk and cereal every which way. Slammed into Bib's already sizable body, taking him down and halfway out the kitchen door. He was already punching me hard in the head as we slid. Two of the bigger boys pulled me off of him, and I slugged one of them and got pounded into the floor by the other like a clean new ten penny nail." There is something extra in his eyes at this point, and … a turn in one corner of his mouth?

"It went on from there, but not well for me, and by the time I was pinned down good, I felt like every one of my six other brothers (not counting Steve) had gotten in a good lick or two on me." I waited for something from Ray. Like I was done.

"That it?" he says again. This time with maybe just a note of disappointment.

"I did not win that fight, nor any within the family, not ever. And my youngest sister lives in that same room to this day. Vera never remarried cause the boys wouldn't allow it, and she lived there too until the day she died."

Ray sits forward, just a little. "What's the point," he asks, and not sarcastically, as far as I can tell.

"No point. Unless you like hearing about me taking a beating?"

"A beating would be good right about now," he smiles. It is a good smile. And he takes it with him as he heads for the door.

• • •

Later, at the motel, I thought about what I was doing with Ray. Not winning any awards, that was for sure. But it looked to me like he was more relaxed, and maybe even not actually hostile. I thought it'd be worth another shot, and I put my own distaste for sharing my private thoughts on hold. Besides, who was he going to tell?

My eye caught a brochure on the cheap desk about nearby Morro Bay, up the Cabrillo Highway from the motel and on the other side of Camp Snoopy. It occurred to me that I could not camp out with Ray, even if he wanted me to, which he certainly did not, and if I was going to make this into an expedition, I would have to find other things to occupy my time, and preferably my thoughts. I drove north.

I was immediately struck at a distance by the overwhelming presence of a great volcanic plug the brochure called Morro Rock rising hundreds of feet above the water of the Bay. It and eight other volcanic plugs are called The Nine Sisters and run in a chain stretching along the highway I'd just driven to get to the Bay. The last of the chain is actually submerged off the coast.

The thought of the sub-mantle activity and the submerged extinct volcano sent me reeling back into my own tectonic history and stopped me short. To what great place had I steered my life's course. Into what great achievement had I so far parlayed all my fortunes, both ill and otherwise. Maybe nowhere. And certainly not much. Not a home to leave, or to return to. And not much of a purpose. Ha. That word again. The one I'd been sneering at for a long time.

But now ... a granddaughter. And maybe now, Eileen. Again. And Clayton Ray.

So maybe there was something to Charles Artemis Bird. Maybe something was about to change.

I parked near the beach and walked out on the white sands to the call of sea birds and the sub-sonic grinding of the machineries of the planet, and up to the sheer granite face of the Rock, grandiosely and locally known as the Gibraltar of the Pacific, even though the real Gibraltar is folded limestone sediment resting on a totally different plate. I placed both of my palms on the weathered rock, and craned my head to look upward, listening.

The planet's solid crust was billions of years old. Solid, but always in motion. And over many hundreds of millions of years that I knew of, it had gone from a spread of continents to a single continent, Pangaea. And then slowly, so slowly no living thing then would ever have had a sense of it, continental forces broke it apart. Most of the parts now almost inconceivably distant from one another. Distant, and usually much shifted in latitude. Much shifted. Maybe in one lifetime I might make such a shift myself.

It's not as if I were a continent.

I stayed for dinner at a harborside restaurant, and learned much of this local geology from a friendly waitress with more time than occupied tables. She was maybe a bit past what she probably thought of as her middle years, grey wisps just showing in the dark brunette hair she had pulled back and away from her face, but there was something about her, some kind of strength, and her obvious health, that drew more from me than a polite glance or two. And she asked a lot about me, my business in town (which I did not share, exactly), what I liked. She helped me choose a seafood dish that was delicious, and by the time I was having coffee and some kind of custard she also recommended, I knew only a little about her. Her name was Rena, she was local, loved the beach and pretty much had never been anywhere else. She told me about volcanic plugs, submerged seamounts, and more history of the area than I thought I would be able to remember, both ancient and human. A kind of tectonic kinship, I thought. No one seemed to mind her taking so much time with me. I didn't mind either. I thanked her, left a generous, but not suggestive, tip and left, a thought submerged about asking when she got off that did not surface until I got back to my room.

• • •

In the interview room again, Ray was waiting for me, standing by his chair. There was no smile to greet me, only those watchful eyes in the darkness of an ancient face. Just maybe a reduction in wariness. I thought that might do. And I wasn't ready to do fist bumps and bro hugs with him anyway.

All there was for me was to win Ray over. Even though that path was not illustrated for me with any particular visions, either at the end, or along the way. It would all just be recon. I was hoping he'd think so too. If, like I wanted him to do, I told the tale I'd never told, couldn't tell.

He sat down. I looked down at my feet, at the floor under them. At what lay under the floor. My own long silent pool of memory. A pool deep and sunken, locked far beneath the plates that made up the crust of my world. Heavier than the rock that surrounded it.

With my stomach turning over, my guts in a cramp, I told it. Like I was drawing up water from that pool. Dark water, heavy, thick and still.

In the dead of winter I was trained to shoot on sight. Identify the enemy and kill him. If necessary at close range, with the edge of a knife. In lessons with mock targets and blunted knife hand-to-hand training exercises. Bloodless. The picture of combat, the unknowable, supposed to be always behind my eyes. All unreality, all adrenaline, all hoping it would never have to be me. Denying the ever blossoming lust to put that training into effect, ashamed of it, frightened of its power, just a little breathless at a distant thrill I could not yet imagine. While I sweated inside my frost coated field gear.

In none of that training, did I see life go out of a person. Suddenly, irrevocably. In none of those exercises, in none of my reluctant reach to foresee actual fighting, did I see the light go out of a pair of eyes. Light taken by me, and squandered.

When I got to the jungle months later I just didn't think about that anymore. When we weren't on patrol, it was like we weren't in a war. Sort of. In it, but not in it. When we were out, and the stink and the bugs owned us body and soul, there were too many other things to think about. Like, not dying today. I was still not thinking about it when they sent us out on another night mission. They called it an 'Interdiction,' a word that made it sound like some kind of corporate business. Maybe it was.

It was to happen on a trail G2 was sure they were using, so we were ordered to set up an ambush. And we did. Our positions, fields of fire. Pretty much by the book. Then we settled in to wait. The Sarge'd had us wash before the mission, wash off our GI insecticide, our GI sweat, all of which he said the Gooks could smell downwind from 300 yards. We didn't wash our gear. Not exactly. I guess the stream crossings were supposed to take care of that. We got dropped 20 klicks from the target, and humped ourselves through mud and streams and sweat and a thousand man-eating bugs and more mud. When we were dug in, upwind as best we could tell, and the claymores set to pop, we may have smelled like the stink of this carnivorous jungle, but we sure didn't smell like what we were. Killers.

I had a bad feeling. Either we would sit for days and get sucked dry by the wildlife, gradually starve from eating nothing but rice, and explode from constipation – or the bastards would slide down the trail like ghosts in the darkness, and die. But not alone – they would take some of us with them.

We did wait for days, and it did get bad, very bad. I think some of us were never right in the head after that. Your mind starts playing tricks, very bad tricks. You hear things, your own crawling sweat feels like the final invasion of small beasts that will sting and devour you. The sound of the jungle gets into your head like a living thing, never to leave again. You forget when you got here, you forget where you came from. You totally forget why. If there had ever been a why. And you cannot stop thinking you are going to die, horribly.

And maybe you take just a moment to feel sad. At the waste of it. With nothing else to be done.

At what I later pieced together as about 3 a.m., and with no warning, all those thoughts, and the rags of some fitful sleep, were shredded with the first blast of claymore detonations. Automatic fire, phosphorus flares, men yelling, screaming. In English and in Vietnamese. The squad I was dug in with was in a cut-off deployment, meant to catch escapees, so they had not yet opened fire. I got my medipac in front of me, expecting any second to hear cries of 'medic!'

Then the night-blackened greenery crashed to pieces in front of me and muzzle flashes lit up the darkness all around me, and I swung up my weapon, all instinct. I could distantly hear the crack and rattle of the squad ripping into the fleeing child-sized soldiers, but all I could see in a tunnel of my own silence was the smudged and boyish face of the man now six feet in front of me. In slow motion, he turned his own weapon on me, complete surprise registered on his face – or I imagined that – but no fear. Riveted breathless to his eyes, I shot him three times.

And light and life vanished. In a single beat of my heart.

His eyes never left me as I spoke, and his face by turns grew looser and then more solemn. Faint nods at points, sometimes a quirk in his left eye. A hard edge to his face would come and then leave – a trick of the light perhaps. His breath not changing at all.

Now I sit slumped at the table, like carelessly dumped refuse.

It was a mistake to bring up this recollection, a mistake to share it with this man I do not know, this man I cannot imagine being related to, in any way. And for what. I feel my feet sinking into the linoleum of this room that we are neither of us present to now.

This room, a tomb I share with Clayton Ray, fills with the slow thump of a fading pulse, and I wish that I were alone in it. That I would never again have to look up and into the eyes of this man, or any other.

10

Iraq. Al Anbar Province.
_/_/2007. The Present.

Blake and the Rug. It's not enough we have to deal with this miserable heat, with hostiles you can't tell from the friendlies. With sand in everything. And the chance of being blown up every time you turn around. No, I get to have a certifiable psycho in my face, a guy who only has to think something and it's done.

I find myself wishing we were moving out, right now, into some kind of shit storm. Where there's nothing to think about. Where both Blake and Rivers might just get theirs.

It creeps me out the way they act, talk, when they are not looking down the sights of their M16s. There is something – off – about them. For one thing, they're both PSC embeds, not Marines. Or at least not anymore. PSCs – those are personal security contractors, and they bring a lot of ex-Rangers, Special Ops and other tough guys in for big bucks, and mostly they don't answer to the chain of command. These two do, sort of I guess, but I think that's because they are embedded in our unit. Don't ask me why, it's above my paygrade. But it sucks. If they ever were (and they don't like to say), they're not Marines now. And I don't think anybody or anything should be mixed in with Marines. They hang out together, and they look at the rest of us, when they look at us at all, like – well – like we are not human. I mean, like they'd do something, anything at all, to any one of us, and maybe for no reason. I just want them gone.

This place is getting to me, I guess.

Blake has fixed up the prayer rug we stole so he can sit on it in the shade and smoke. Rivers is usually there with him, and some of the others. Guys who want to be like them. I don't like to go near that rug, and like I said, not being around Blake always seems like a good idea. Today they are rolling up some weed they've scored and they are already a little messed up on something else. They are laughing that group laugh of theirs. One of them spills something on the rug and Rivers jumps up and shoves the guy over and the guy's free hand lashes out and smacks the guy next to him and there's grunting and words, and Blake stands up, almost ceremonially, unzips and takes a wiz on the rug, right next to where the other two are wrestling.

"Hey!" yells the guy Rivers shoved. "What the fuck are you doing, asshole!"

"I'm cooling you hotheads off," Blake says lazily, finishing and zipping up.

Everybody over there laughs and settles down to their smoke break again, except nobody wants to sit where Blake has relieved himself.

I am so mad I want to shoot all of them. "You know," I start in on them, "the least you fuckers could do would be to show some respect for the family you stole that rug from." I feel the rest coming, and I try to hold it back, but can't. "Y'all make me sick. Maybe I should take that rug back to that village." And I turn away from them and spit in the sand. It's not enough to get the taste of urine and shame and temper out of my mouth.

Blake and Rivers exchange looks, and Blake says, easy – like he's just telling us all that he's going down to the BX to pick up some smokes – he says, "You know, Bird." He looks at me steadily. "We did that family, and the Corps, a lot of good when we hosed 'em all down. Cut down on the population of psychotic filth out here. They had it coming. And a lot more, if we'd had time … " he lets his words trail off suggestively, eyeing the others, as if to say, 'Know what I'm sayin'?' Their agreement is plain, and silent.

"So, Birdman, you can get off your wagon load of shit," punching the word 'wagon load', he stands quickly, fluidly, and in two steps has one arm over my shoulder, in a vicious play on being buds. Bending down just a little, like being eye to eye with me, he lets a small smile flicker on his lips, and goes on, "and come down over here and smoke some gange with us like a brother, or … ?" Again the suggestive look around to, and the unspoken agreement from, the pukes. "Or, we can make other arrangements, about you, and maybe do the Corps some good that way too?" He grins and letting my shoulder go, claps me briskly on the back, hard enough to make the dust rise.

That's it for me. I am ready to end this whack job right now. I knock his arm aside, hard enough to leave a mark, I hope, and I exhale and set myself. My guard ready to rise if he takes the challenge. He shows no sign of pain in his arm, or even anger. He continues to look at me closely, like the insect he thinks I am. I wonder if he is figuring whether I am worth the effort. I hope he is figuring whether he actually can just do what he wants to me, like he was suggesting.

I hope he can see how much I would like to empty him out. And he does. I can tell. And now his smile is genuine. Cold. The others can see the sport in the air between us and there are some low calls of 'oooo', 'wooo', 'ohhh' that are smothered pretty quick in response to all of us seeing a visible tick in the side of Blake's neck. And we stay like that, nobody moves, and the air between us gets even hotter than the desert has already made it.

"Oh no, I do Not smell some old rope burning," we all hear the Gunny saying as he comes around the corner. "Anybody got time for some pollution, got time to take care of some other pollution I Know needs taking care of." And he stops, squared off to us. Looking for challenge. There is none.

11

Iraq. Al Anbar Province
_/_/2007. The Present.

"You think a dream like that means anything?" I asked her, after I had that – thing – in the jungle stream, and everybody thought I was crazy.

Antibbe Marks is a piece of work. She is bent over the scattered parts of her weapon, micro-inspecting every millimeter of each piece, touching one with a soft oiled cloth here, a fingernail flick or a puff of her breath there. We don't talk much, mostly because I think she does not like to talk. At least not to any of us in the platoon. But she does not fuck with your head, and sometimes she is maybe the only one I can talk to. Like right then.

"Means whatever you think it means." She reflects back to me. Typical, real short. Her weapon practically reassembles itself, as if by magic.

The other week we were all hanging out, and Sergeant Fitz busts in on us, wanted us out for special patrol jump-off double time and he shouts, "I want every stiff dick outa here in 65 seconds!" Marks is not moving fast enough for him and he prowls over to her, stops next to her. I catch this little sorta smile on her face he can't see.

He gets right up in her face and says, almost nice, "Do you, Marks? Have a stiff dick?"

Still moving like slack tide in an estuary, she gives him, "For you Sergeant? Always."

That's what I'm talking about.

Later I overheard some of the guys we call the Dirty Third talking about Marks – how they should bang some sense into her. I couldn't help it. These are the guys who like to hang with Blake and Rivers. Who sit on that defiled rug with them. I went up and said, "You guys think you can separate Marks from the rest of this platoon?"

A guy we call Minnow answers, "What'sa matter Bird, you want in on it? Or are you already 'in' and wanna keep us out?" Large smiles and knowing head nods all around. Assholes.

"You try anything and you'll answer to every Marine in the unit." I can't believe I said that. Then I went and told her about that, and also about what Blake said to me, just before the Gunny interrupted us.

"I can't believe you said any of that," she tells me. "Sometimes I wonder which of us is more hopeless."

So I am pressing her again about this, well, I am calling it a dream. Even though that's not what it felt like. Not getting anywhere either, like trying to shovel sand out of a hole. "I mean, so much detail," I tell her, "like I was really there. Like it was really me."

She shrugs. Then cocks, sights and dry fires her weapon, and starts to strip it down again.

"You think I got a screw loose?"

"I think that about everybody here, including me."

"You think I might be losing it?"

She doesn't say anything to that, doesn't look like she's thinking about it either. She gets the whole weapon apart again, pokes at the recoil spring as if it shouldn't be there. "No. I don't." She says, as if to herself. "But that don't mean you aren't."

• • •

You never know who shares your bivouac - psychopaths? Or Navy Cross heroes.

I read about one guy who chose not to accept his medal and to remain unknown so he could stay in his unit. The Corps won't say who he is out of respect for his wishes. He and maybe a dozen others like him. I don't know about the hero thing. Seems pretty arbitrary to me. Guy steps up, like we all do sometimes, lays it down and gets a medal. Not something any of us are holding our breath for. Still. That guy could be right here. Could be Benton, f'chrissakes.

And then there's Blake and Rivers. Total psychos. Right?

Nobody here is your plain average Joe, or Joan, for that matter. Maybe it's being here. Maybe it started in boot camp. Still, the Marines I fight beside seem like mostly good people. Take Benton, whether or not he's got a medal. Squirrely little guy, hard as a rock, but not a tough guy, if you know what I mean. And you never know what he's been reading, or thinking about. Funny as hell. Except when he's serious. Never backs down, gives it to you straight — you couldn't ask for someone better to have your back.

And Marks? Go figure for her. Good looking woman, trim build, don't know how she survived boot, but she did, and more than that. I hear she's top marks at hand-to-hand combat, at least the kind that doesn't involve actual wrestling. Real smart too, plus she takes no shit, never complains. About heat, sand, long treks with heavy packs, nothing. I wonder how many other Marines of the female persuasion are basically in her boots.

Because you have Lance Corporal Pidelski over in another platoon. She's got a hard-on for the men in our platoon. Which is funny when you think of it. You might think Bernadette Pidelski would have trouble getting it up. But oh Baby. If any guy does not have his Shit squared away around her? That guy is going to learn some new ways to hurt. No one says anything to her face. Anymore. I heard about a guy? On a base in the rear, acting like he was back in the world, come on to her. Nothing serious, I heard. Just fooling around they said. She moved in close to him, all 5 foot 6 inches of her and looked up into his face with a smile on her lips, and when he bent down to what he thought was an obvious invitation, she smashed her forehead into his nose and lips, swept his rear leg and jumped on his knee. And when she had him down like that, she started kicking him in the ribs, the gut and the face. Dumb shit thought the sky fell on him. He is back in the world now, with a limp.

She did two weeks in the brig for that but they didn't bust her down. She came out of the can looking for more. I hear she got raped. Somewhere, back in the day, maybe even after she joined up. It's rough on women. It's not right. But nobody's worried right now about Pidelsky – they're worried about us. Seems like she's not just out to make sure there are no further misunderstandings about if and when she chooses a partner for that kind of dance – she's out to make sure there are no shitheads left to ask. And we are all scum to her.

So it's weird to be out on an op with her. You can't help thinking she'd just as soon shoot you, or let one of the rebels do it for her. But it's not that way. And more than one of us guys is still walking around swinging because she did the right thing at the right time. Seems the safest you can be around her is on patrol, in a fight.

So like I say, you never know. About that.

• • •

No, you never know. About that. Or anything really. I mean we're Marines, right? Not supposed to care, or get involved.

Just Mission. But really? When we fought the insurgents and dug in and then went house to house, to take back that city for its own citizens, even when the Brass thought it was a bad idea? Is what I heard. And the Super Brass wanted it done anyway?

We did it. We just did it.

And some of us – I mean some of us didn't make it. No, a lot of us. Good Marines spent their lives. God Damn it! It makes me so mad! We did all that? For nothing?

The rebels get stronger and their actions more savage, and then we're attacked by those same citizens whose city we saved, and the Top Brass says to just let it all go, give it back to them? Suffering Jesus. How can a guy make any sense of it?

Everything we fought for - just taken away. The plan was shitty to begin with, not a plan at all really – even squad level guys like me could see that. And then it's 'shut it down – gather it up and move out'?

Sent in for nothing.

Maybe that's what there is to know.

12

Eight legs suspended above the floor, thinnest thread disappearing upward. The creature works his line, pulling, gathering. He stops to rest, or assess, his thoughts unreadable to me, perhaps spinning themselves out into another dimension. He begins again to climb. And slip.

No hazard prompts his struggle except perhaps eventual starvation, no panic drives him in his relentless, if not hopeless, effort for small gains, soon lost. An inch or so, then a slip half way back, then up a fraction again to slip an inch and a half. He stops, multiple questing limbs reasoning the job.

I sit and watch, so large and vastly apart from him that I am beyond his notice. And I wonder if God sits and watches me? And if I, consumed by my own climbs and slips, am also lost to any knowledge or sense of being watched?

His thread is stirred by faint breezes, my own senses too course to find them. He sways, suspended like a lazy trapeze, too sleepy to perform. A chance encounter with an age-worn curtain and the swaying stops, the passenger disembarks his filamentous ride, quickly scurries up and around the edge of the fabric. 'Good,' I think. Good for him.

This spider to my Walt Whitman.

I am suspended in my own efforts to climb and become. Perhaps I sway too in breezes I cannot sense. Pull, stretch, yearn, fear. Slip. Rest and assess. And blame and cry out. And despair. Except maybe for the pull and slip, I would put all of these into a different dimension, one to which I have no access. I cannot endure the blame, the fear. I would be free of reaching. And despair. I look up along my own probable course, I cannot see its end.

Then a different wind stirs my courage, or my anger, and I tighten my grip, heave what strength I have been given, and rise again.

From around a corner of material, the creature emerges, onto the glassy surface of the tiled wall, safety line still attached to somewhere above. The traverse is interrupted at intervals with the predictable slip, a short fall, the catch of thread, the recovery. And onward.

San Luis Obispo
_/_/2007. The Present.

I know I have it or something like it to do again. Last night, in Ray's prison? Sitting with him, drawing from that ... pool.

I cannot think how I will do it. I cannot think what compels me. Tuyet? Looking at me, even now, with her luminous eyes, her simple command to me a frightening comfort? Or Ray's own gravitational pull? There's that. Or have I caught the edge of something. A fracture. A fault. The beginning of a new continent.

Something I cannot do if I stay dead. Dead. I have been staying dead, a long time.

Maybe I should go first into Morro Bay again, find that place, maybe the waitress. Rena?

I go into the bathroom, avoid the mirror.

No shave today.

I remember somebody telling us, when we were cherries, in Vietnam, when the first mortar round landed near us and I am sure we all shit our pants. The look on his face, the look on ours. I remember him telling us just to forget about living through the war. "Forget about it. You're all scared because you think there is still something ahead you don't want to lose. Well, there isn't. You're already dead."

It sounded sick to me then. A horrible idea. And it scared me badly. I did not want to die – I couldn't even think about dying. Everyday I went through a litany of what my life really was, back in the world, what I would do when I got back. Who I would see. What I would make of myself. No. I couldn't die.

I don't remember when that changed.

I guess I just thought less and less about my future. Thought more about just getting through the night. And the next day. Scared all the time, and bullshitting everybody about how tough I was. I guess the whole string of days and nights, shelling, shooting, patching up the living, holding the dying. The endless hours, days, the waiting ... for some suspended thing to happen. I guess the whole thing just came to seem like already being dead, like the guy said. It wasn't something I decided or chose. Wasn't even something I thought about. Or said. One day I just realized that I was doing what the guy told us to do. I forgot about being alive. Somewhere along the way, on a dark trail, crossing a stream, wading through some muck.

I guess that was the same as being dead.

It changes you. It does make you strong when everything screams at you to run, panic, get hysterical, fight for your life. Makes you strong so you can fight - to do what you have to do. And then maybe later, even much later, long after it is all over, you can think of not being already dead. You can live and expect to live. To move on from being dead. And leave behind what is dead to you. Much later.

And what about the part of me that will never want to give up that particular and unique strength?

• • •

I drive down the highway along The Nine Sisters and out to Morro Rock again. With my palms flat against its flanks and my head tilted back, I connect again with the deep processes of the earth. Through the salt air and the cries of birds, my lungs, my bones, reverberate with the ultra low frequencies of the heart of this living thing, this great planet. It is a settling kind of meditation, though I cannot say I have ever or otherwise made a practice of such interior processes.

My new 'friend' at the harborside restaurant is not on until 3pm, so I go back to the prison. Willing, if not ready, to try once more to make a bridge over to Ray.

I am the first in the room and an escort officer I recognize sticks his head in and gives me a sign, then ducks out to be replaced by Ray.

"I get it man," he smiles in the doorway. "You do not have to go on with the soul searching. I still do not want to talk about it, what you are after. You can get that from my niece, but I appreciate what you are doing. Ok?"

"Yeah, ok with me." I step around to the other side of the table and indicate the empty chair. "Will you sit down anyway?" I wait, hand extended. Like it is easy and I am happy to wait all day for it.

He moves over and sits down. The smile has pulled back in, his face is once again empty. He studies me.

"So is there anything you want to tell me now, before I go see your niece?"

"Yeah," he says. "I know what that took for you to tell me. And I think it would be fair for me to open up a little with you." He looks at me. "And I can't."

It's a fact for him. That's all.

"Ok," I say, standing up, my hand out. "See you later?"

I think he is not going to take my offered hand. Then he does. It is a good hand.

"Ok," he says.

Los Angeles
_/_/2007. The Present.

Louise Carter. Ray'd already told me her name and where to find her, said he'd sent word and told her I was coming. So I guess I am driving down to see if I can find out from her what the world looked like to young Clayton long ago.

I find her at her mother's place in Compton. She meets me at the door, offers me her hand and invites me in. She has coffee and cookies waiting for us at a low table in the living room. We exchange names, and she motions me to sit in an armchair with doilies, but it is very awkward. I cannot make small talk. She is a pleasant featured woman of middle years. And her eyes are large with expectation. I just jump in.

"Clayton tells me you write a lot to him. Visit too."

She looks relieved to have something to say. "I do. I know Mama doesn't like to hear about it now, but she's mostly in the back anyway, sick a lot of the time. Broke her heart when Uncle Clayton was convicted. He told me you were coming down, but he didn't say why." She looks the question at me. Her face is open, genuine, but not yet friendly.

"I have a lot of questions. You know I am trying to find out what happened back then in Vietnam? What happened to Clayton Ray?"

She nods slightly.

"Well, I have visited him several times now, and I thought it would help if I knew more about his life. His early life." I wait. She says nothing and shows no sign for me either to stop or to continue. "He said he didn't want to talk about that anymore, but I could ask his sister. Or you."

This time my wait is answered. "Oh. Yes. Well, like I said, Mama doesn't talk much these days, and I'm sure she doesn't want to talk about her brother Clayton. Not now." She moves her coffee cup, pushes the plate of cookies around a bit, sits back in the couch, looks out the window and crosses her knees. "What can I tell you?"

She tells me a lot, and I thank her the best I can, even take a cookie with me when I go. It is enough for me to see that there are many more questions to ask about this man, and not enough, not near enough, to provide all the answers, especially about that day in 1970.

Clayton Ray was the second youngest of eleven children. Just like me. His sister Emelda is eight years older than him. He was born in 1951 (also like me) in Bakersfield where his father was working in the oil fields as a roughneck. They moved soon after that to find work in West Texas (possibly even near me at the time?) and stayed there until 1962 when his father was killed in an oilfield accident. They moved to LA, and Emelda, her mom and six of the younger children ended up in a place in Watts. Emelda and her mom and a few of the older six did what they could to make their way, and Clayton found his way onto the streets. Louise said Emelda had told her all about this part many times.

Young Ray was smart, likeable and tough. And he was soon running with a gang of black radicals, all of whom were a lot older than him. Louise didn't know a lot about that part because he would not discuss it with Emelda who was mostly terrified that he would be hurt or killed, and begged him over and over to stay in school and learn how to get along in the world. Louise said Emelda did remember his reply to that plea, and would often repeat it to Louise, especially after he was drafted and got in so much trouble and was on trial for his life.

"Get along in the world?" he'd said. "You mean get down on my knees and kiss Whitey's ass?!" He'd shouted angrily, usually punctuated by slamming or throwing something. "Get along?! Like our father?! 'Yassuh. Nosuh. Please suh, can I work masef to death to put money in your stinking white hands'?! Do you even see what is going on here? Right in front of you? We work for scraps that fall off the white man's table and we kill each other over them!" Emelda had tried to downplay his ferocious response to her when relating this memory to Louise, but Louise had guessed correctly about the depths of her uncle's passion.

When the riots came to Watts in 1965 Clayton was only 14, but he had been a leader in some of the worst of the fighting. Had gotten arrested more than once, and beaten savagely. And he'd stayed active in neighborhood causes, activism and fights with authority after the smokes had dissipated over South LA.

When he got his draft notice in late 1969, Louise told me he tore it up in front of his family and said "I'm going to fight all right, but not against some Asian brothers who are also trying to throw the white man out." His mom and Emelda both begged him repeatedly not to refuse, to go and fight in the army and in the end, he'd agreed.

And I can not tell from her story why he did.

Two

Vietnam - 1970

Quick feet move in relative silence against a deafening background of night jungle sounds. Not a wash of white noise like river rapids or ocean surf, but a great factory of sounds manufactured in alien overtones and layers. Sounds like thousands of ceaselessly moving tiny pulleys and chains all badly in need of grease, like hundreds of dull thin masonry bits each drilling into its own block of concrete, like countless hollow wooden washboards each scraped frantically back and forth with a dry bone. And like a rush of pebbles cascading down over rows and rows of glass bottles laid on their sides. Sounds like these. Impossibly mixed with the more familiar sounds of chirping crickets.

Arms covered with soft cloth part heavy damp leaves so two keen eyes, shaded from the overhead glare, can see across the compound and the lights that burn all night. As blatant as the ancient fires that primitives fueled to keep the predators of the night at bay, and no more effective. The hooch for new officers is plainly visible and made distinct from the others by its lack of surrounding recreational clutter, by rope lines and canvas planes just that much tauter, flatter than those of the enlisted men.

Getting around behind the quarters will be easy, obscured in the perimeter for a while longer. From there making lazy unconcerned movements from the edge of the compound to the screening on the hut will attract no particular attention from the listless sentries.

Released by those arms, the leaves flow back together as the feet glide away, covered by the din of that jungle sound factory.

At the officers' hooch two ears listen for the night sounds of sleeping men, hear the aimless scrape of boots on wooden flooring. Bedtime chores perhaps? Or the restless walk of the fearful? This late at night there should be no further trips to the latrine, at least not until much later, when drink has had its chance to move from gullet to groin. Even if they are not all asleep, it is time.

The waffle-studded exterior of the vaguely double-coned, pineapple shaped ordnance slips easily from the large trouser pocket, and nimble fingers quickly wire its neck to the door handle. A last look around, a final pause to listen for activity *within, and one hand reaches to steady the door and its attached charge and to hold the spoon to its body, while the other hand deftly, almost gently, pulls out the safety pin and ring and drops them into a pocket. No sounds. No change. Good.*

Release the spoon, and a small ting-tack sound is swallowed in the background of jungle sounds. And the hands, the eyes and the feet disappear quickly into the night, only the ears present to the very faint hiss of a defective Russian fuse.

13

I've been hearing the sound all morning in my sleep. In, and out, of my sleep. A sound I thought I had forgotten. I remember now. The sound I promised I'd never have to hear again.

In my dream it was deathly quiet. Not even those usually constant night sounds. We lay under shelter halves, expecting more rain, eyes searching the dark, ears straining.

Then it found me.

A low animal sound. At first. Stabbing into my hurt, my own terror. Insinuating into my own thought-emptied head. A warble, cut off, then another. Two, then three.

O God. Whimpers.

Children. Crying children.

• • •

When I got out ... from all the recovery. From everything. From the long tunnel leading away from my tomb in the mud. From death everywhere. I was just ... done. It was all gone. They were all dead. To me.

Not just Tuyet. All those guys I had sewn up, saved. And the ones I did not. The land, the smells, the people. The sounds. All dead and gone. And I never thought of them. Not once. Not even when the very rare letter or card caught up with me at some hospital. I left them unread. Unopened.

So I never found out about my unit doing a number on some vil, supposed to be a VC stronghold. Never heard about the flag. The one they were all so proud of.

Except. Somehow I did know. Not details. Maybe I just made something up. At night. When sleep would not come. Or when it did, it did not come alone. The dreams. Terrible dreams that I would forget when I woke up. Except. Sometimes, I do remember ... something.

There comes a kind of intrusion, a slither. Daytime, anytime. A fading of eyesight. And then clarity. Monstrous, horrific clarity. A cry driven from my chest, a ripping in my heart. I throw up my hands and arms to cover my face, as if it comes at me, from somewhere outside. I cry and scream. And beg. Until it has passed.

I know nothing like that happened while I was there. Right? Not to my unit. I'd remember. I would. Wouldn't I? I know it did happen, sometimes, some places. But not to us. Did it? No. Not by us.

No.

Smackover, Arkansas
_/_/2007. The Present.

I can't stop thinking that Ray's bitterness must be rooted in the injustice of his treatment as a young man, and then as a black soldier in Vietnam (and God knows what after that). That while he may have thought of killing his CO, maybe even wanted to, wanted him dead – like nearly everyone else wanted him dead? That he had not done the act. And yet he alone had been singled out for persecution.

I am telling myself it is for the sake of Tuyet, though I only half believe it. I can tell there is something else there, something I cannot deny I feel for this aggravating and puzzling man. Something I do not want to talk about. Or think. I've become determined to vindicate him at every possible level, even to find the actual killer after all this time. God willing.

And since I cannot face him again, or at least not right now, since I cannot go and ask him more questions – which he would probably refuse to answer anyway – things for me maybe to go on, I start looking somewhere else.

When I first started getting my kill money, the money, the disability pay the Army sends to me every month for in fact not dying, for basically being only about half shot away, I never wanted to touch it. And I never have. I saved up the first 10-12 checks that came while I was in hospitals, and put it all in an account and changed my VA records to have the money sent to that account every month. And when I was in deep shit for more than 20 years I never looked at it. Only now, after Tuyet sent me off. It wasn't that much per month, but I guess it's true what they say. Savings add up.

That's what I am using now. Plane tickets, motels. I've even thought of hiring a PI. But somehow that doesn't seem like the right way to go.

I am starting with Army records, which are a shit-hole of their own. But they can also be a gold mine for me. All it takes is time ... and money. So? I have the money. God Bless Uncle Sam for that. And

God knows I have the time. Who knows. This may be the best plan yet for not losing it – my mind, again. For staying out of … the dark places.

• • •

And now I've confirmed that Ray's unit shared the base with ours during the time of the fragging. I think there must still be some of the fellows from his unit who remember the loudly outspoken and often censured black soldier who was young Clayton Ray. I've confirmed that the deadly hooch had indeed been intended for Ray's CO, company commander Captain Inaugieu and that the three LTs that night had been last minute substitutes. And that as far as Army records could provide, neither of the two men that died could have been known in any way by any of the men on the base. And that the officer who survived, though he'd been in Vietnam longer, was down from a totally different division and must have been unknown to the men on that base that night.

I decide to begin with Captain Inaugieu and Army records put me on his trail, with the Smackover, Arkansas Chamber of Commerce pinpointing him for me. (They also tell me that the original French settlers called the area *Sumac Couvert* – French for covered in dense sumac vegetation – but that the later land grant settlers anglicized it to Smackover.)

He wasn't in his office, so I find him at home and tell him I'm writing a long overdue follow-up on the fragging and hope to report his side. He's reluctant.

"Having that shit happen on my watch would've been bad enough to put a crimp in my career. But that damn Ray getting acquitted, despite my report and testimony? I didn't find out about that until my tour was up and I was back stateside."

"When was that?"

"Oh? Hell, that was forty years ago. I don't recall. Maybe late 1971, early 72? Anyway, when I did some checking around on my record, my review boards, when I first got passed over for Major? There it all was. Like dogshit tracked all over my carpet. I was finished. You say you're going to print all this? My side of it?"

"Well, yes sir, I will write it up and present it – I can't guarantee it will get printed like I write it."

"I don't know." He rubs his palm back and forth over his still short and bristly hair as he paces, then heads out to his kitchen and opens the fridge door. "Y'all want a beer?"

I thank him but decline and he pops the top and comes back in sipping it.

"Sonovabitch," he mutters under his breath. "Ok. Here's what it was. That bastard was not the first of his kind to come into my unit and cause trouble."

"His kind?" I ask. "You mean black?"

"Black, white, Latino? What's the difference?" He gives me what I can only call a mean glare.

"No – you don't be putting any of that racist shit on me, boy. I'll throw your sorry ass out of here right now! Get me?!"

My own anger flares suddenly, and I want him to do just that. Throw me out. Or try. Boy. I want to take him apart. I can feel the violence rising from my forearms up past my heart, into my head. My vision is sharpening, my breath gets short.

I think of Tuyet and oddly I think about the tea, and I take a conscious breath, hold up a palm and tell him, "No offense meant, sir. I want to write the best story I can. And that means getting clear on every possible point." I wait, looking at him. "Do you want me to continue?"

He palms his hair again. "Ok, yeah. Sure. I just don't want any misunderstandings. Ok?"

"Neither do I." My inner vision still has us both going down the steps, me shoving something into his guts. I never imagine my own injuries. Until too late.

"Alright then." He catches a breath. "He comes in there, to my camp, and first thing he does is start in yellin' about white bastards this and fuckin Army that. And I had Top go out and shut him up, right off. Had his ass hauled into my office. I tell him what was what, and if he doesn't want to spend his entire tour locked up in a hole somewhere, he damn better shut his trap. And he gives me this ... look. Black Power, I guessed. I knew right then where we were going with this guy." He gives me his own look and holds it on me awhile.

I have to keep my eyes on my notes so he won't read in those same eyes the truth I feel about him. "So, what then?"

"So – and hey, his implied threat didn't bother me any, it wasn't my first rodeo, know what I mean? He and ten other grunts, at any one time, wanted me dead. Sure felt like it. I told him to go get his shit straightened out, and be standing tall in formation in the morning for inspection. Look, I wasn't real worried about threats because I always made sure there were no live rounds loose when anybody came back in from an op, no grenades. I mean hell, we weren't in danger of an attack. I had standing orders that the men were to draw what they'd need on the way out to every mission.

"Anyway, the next morning he is not even in the formation. Top says his name is on the sick call list, and he is in his bunk, moaning he can't get up. I had two corporals haul his ass out of the hooch and dropped right in front of me, and damn if he didn't just puke all over my boots! It was all I could do right there to not kick his face in, and then draw my sidearm and shoot him dead. God knows I wanted to. I went to clean my boots and told Top to drag his ass over to the infirmary."

And, if there is a God, then he also knows what I want to do to *this* guy, right now.

"And that's how it was with him. The whole time. Right up to the, uh, incident. A malingering, slovenly, disrespectful, sorry-assed soldier. I had him up on a dozen charges and we were gonna can him and ship him back home to be someone else's problem. When that hooch blew up."

"I see," I say, seething, finishing some notes. "So what happened after the explosion and the deaths."

"I knew it was him. I never did figure where he got the grenade. But that kind of thing is always possible if a man wants to really do serious damage. It was a god damn war, you know?"

"Yes. And being in war, did you consider that maybe it was Bed Check Charlie? VC?"

"Of course," he declares, straightening, almost to attention. "It wasn't my first thought, but war is war. I checked with other bases, units like ours. No indication of any VC pattern, and no other VC related fragging incidents reported in the period." He gives me a new look intended to make me feel stupid. Then he slumps back down to his regular self. "Damn shame about those fine boys," shaking his head, a little wobbly from beer he's likely been drinking all day.

"The officers who were killed?"

"Yes – who else!" He lashes at me. "Fine young soldiers. I never got to know them at all." His eyes cast around his place, as if he'd lost something, or was maybe just looking for a place to sit but like someone had moved all the furniture around on him. "I still had to write the letters to their next of kin, as their commanding officer." He gives up his search, looks at me but not squarely. "Later I told them what really happened."

"Really happened?"

"Yes. What that bastard did. And they wrote me back, one of them did, thanking me and asking me to make sure he paid for it. That nothing would ever be enough." The infantry captain's steely glare is in his eye now, and years after Vietnam it is still intimidating to me.

I meet his gaze the best I can. It's like the last defense he has, like there is one true thread left in his life, and it is slipping away from him, even as I watch.

"I failed them. I failed those boys. He never paid a damn thing. I can't stop thinking about that."

I leave him to that, his slow crumble. There's no time for him now – it all stopped decades ago. I know that feeling, have known it well. But as far as

I'm concerned, he set all this in motion on himself and I don't have more of my time for him.

I break in on him, "But you investigated anyway, right? What did you uncover?"

"Uncover? God damn it man, aren't you listening?" Whatever he's reduced to, whatever unlucky destination he's got planned for himself, he knows how to bring flint to the steel in those eyes and spark his anger into bloom. "That place was blown to pieces, Lieutenant Gitridge was damn lucky to survive. Had to medivac him straight out. The others? Gone. Jesus. What an ugly business." His eyes go distant, and his voice comes from that distance. "There wasn't anything to investigate."

I can't help it. I wait for him to return. He looks at me, face red, eyes threaded now with their own crimson degeneration.

"Ray said he'd spent the night with his pals – a bunch of no-goods just like him – and they backed him up. But they'd a done that if I'd a caught him fucking a pig outside my tent. See what I was up against?"

I got nothing to say to that.

He paces some more, palming his head, and goes to get another beer, starts to close the fridge, then has a second thought and holds the can out to me so I can shake my head no.

"Ok. So I had the wreckage sifted, when we had time, and came up with this grenade spoon. Russian. Old model. Piece of crap those old things – just as likely to blow up in your hand as do any damage to an enemy. Must've found the grenade out on patrol and kept it. Smuggled it back to base. Anyway, lots of the guys kept their grenade pins, used them for roach clips." His old eyes begin to gleam balefully with a smothered fire. "But we searched Ray and his pin was from a Russian grenade. Nobody else had anything like that! We had tests run and proved his pin came from that spoon. We had him!"

I do not bring up that later testing by Ray's defense team actually proved that there was no correlation at all between that spoon and that pin. Or that there was testimony that finding the spoon itself in that war-ravaged land did not mean that the fatal grenade had been Russian at all. Only that at least one old Russian grenade had gone off in that area, at some point. What I do bring up is, "Didn't Ray say that he'd found the pin, not a grenade, out on patrol. That there were a bunch of them lying in one place. Probably from some earlier ambush by the VC?"

"Oh yeah, he said that." He had turned away to pace as I made my point, but he spins around on me suddenly, taking a crouch, "Goddam it man! What the hell else would he have said?! Cowardly bastard!" He finds his can empty, tries to crush it but only dents it, throws it at the wall and stalks out to the kitchen muttering.

I pack up my notes to leave. And think about the last 30+ years for this man. Passed over, forced out with no pension, probably in and out of needy relationships, and an insurance career that clearly had no meaning for him. Could Ray – could I – have devised a worse fate for this guy than the one he had dealt himself?

If he'd been the one who died in that hooch, he would've been a hero.

• • •

I stayed around Smackover a few days after that. I wasn't feeling so good. I didn't want another relapse, and I thought maybe I needed to simmer down just a bit. The dreams were starting to come back, and I was flashing a lot on beating the bejesus out of people I'd only just met. Pills didn't seem to help.

In the last dream, a man did some horrible thing, I don't remember what. No one was there except his friends, a woman and two men. I dream of that. Over and over. And I try to stop him, in the dream. I shoot him myself, but he doesn't die. And when he does, I also have to kill his two men friends. One I shoot. And the other I have to try and kill with a dull screwdriver.

• • •

Then I get a call from Inaugieu telling me he remembered the name of a guy in Ray's old platoon. Skinny Planchet. A good fighter he says. Just that he liked to hang around the dopers and misfits.

In Bawcomville just west of Monroe on the Ouachita River in NE Louisiana I find him still serving as a kind of local postmaster on the Jonesboro Road.

"I always liked those boys. They had their heads up their asses, but that was ok with me – was as good a place to look at the war from as anywheres else, right? You was there wasn't you? I see you got the look."

"Yeah, medic. An Khe. Came home early."

"Get shot up?"

"Pretty much."

"So why you asking about Ray now? You know he's in prison, right?"

"I heard some things about him. Kinda getting myself sorted out after all this time, thought it would do me good to think about someone else for a change," I improvise, but I hear some truth in what I'm making up.

He is giving me a surprisingly searching look. "32 years."

"What?" I've missed some shift in what we're talking about.

"32 years, like it don't mean anything. This guy gets a bum rap from way back in the days of the jungle, spends – years – in the brig or whatever they call it. And a miracle happens and he gets off. Some folks saying he did it, but the Army fucked it up in their slobbering rush to pin it on a black guy. I don't know, how the hell would anybody know, except him.

"And then he lives his life – for 32 years – in and out of mental wards, medicated and treated for PTSD, which they didn't even call it that back then – lives this, I don't know, miserable fucking life, for 32 years. And boom. He freaks out one day, beats the ever loving shit out of some bastard probably had it coming, puts him in the hospital, and they arrest him for aggravated. Try him too, only this time no Army screw-ups to get him off. His lawyers plead all kinds of fancy stuff – amounts to temporary insanity – he had PTSD, poor bastard veteran, give him a break, he has a loving family, the guy he pasted is a shit bag – blah blah. And no dice. They nail him for attempted murder and put him away. Does that make any kind of fucking sense?"

The force of his feelings is like a blow. I want to sit down, absorb all of this. I lean a bit closer to him, "No?"

He's run on, almost without waiting for any answer from me. "I never saw him again after they arrested him. Finished my tour, went home. Did my thing here. But I couldn't get him out of my mind. Found out about the trial – it was in lots of papers back then, and then I guess I just made a habit of checking in, asking questions, getting news wherever I could." He turns away and does something with some letters and a few packages, more like a way to be with his thoughts? I leave him alone.

"He gets out in a couple years," he says, not looking up, shuffling mail. "He'll be sixty something. Hauled his black ass off to the jungles and that didn't kill him. Tried him for murder and that didn't work. Pumped him full of experimental drugs for decades, and threw him in the slammer for ten years, and he still ain't dead." He puts down the stuff and takes a step back over toward me. Points a finger at my chest. "I don't know what he is, but he's not dead. You want some of that?"

When I don't answer right away, he turns away again, almost as if I had been the one to leave. He's heading for a doorway in the back of his store, still speaking, but not to me anymore. "Not me, not any of it. I hope he did kill those two bastards in the jungle. It's the only way this all makes any sense."

The only way it makes sense. I need to go see Ray. And then maybe my doc, about my meds? I'm tired but I just can't sleep.

• • •

131

I wake up from another violent dream with my guts screaming. My head crushed in a ring of fire. I fumble around for my meds in a southern pre-dawn in one more strange room, swallow two dry, lay back down and swallow again, and again.

I worked hard in this dream.

It's all gone wrong. Completely wrong. It should not have happened like that. I lie here stunned, halfway back into that dream, or one just like it, struggling to reach some state that made sense and didn't hurt, but only partly getting there. A good man had done a terrible thing, for the right reason. And now he would be the one to pay the price that the rotten bastard he killed should have rightly paid. It's all wrong.

In my dream, this whole thing replayed and replayed. I worked on the wrongness. I changed this and it came out the same, I changed that, and still the same. Like it was hard wired.

Then I put myself in the dream. It was me who crashed into the room, confronting the vigilante about to take out the trash. I made him wait. He wanted to finish his work. I told him he could not, that it was over for him. He screamed that this scum had to be ended – the innocent victim demanded it – that he would only go out and repeat his horrible crime. I told him I agreed. I pleaded. I told him I did not want, could not bear, to see him pay the price for justice. We stayed like that, locked, while the degenerate slobbered hysterically.

I put away my gun. I told this hero to put away his piece and beat it. I told him I would take care of it myself. Not now, but soon.

I worked hard, to make it right.

The violence, the injustice, fills my head constantly. I dream about it. I think about it. Sometimes I condemn myself for it. Why does it fill me? Others don't seem to mind.

And even while I am fixing on it, I see the fault. The slippage. The crack that I will slide down into when I put any of my wishes into action. And it stops me.

But it does not cleanse me.

14

Iraq. Al Anbar Province.
_/_/2007. The Present.

It is night, and the stars shine without a twinkle. Thousands. Millions. We lie against our packs, some in pairs murmuring, most of us alone with our thoughts, and angry fears. There isn't a breath of wind, the sand is like a carpet.

Benton whispers loudly, "Fuck it. Fuck it, man."

WillieG whispers in response, "What?"

T-Bone croaks, "Whatchu on about, B?"

"Fuck it." Benton rolls to sit up, scrapes his helmet down over his forehead. "We never get our own."

Nobody says anything, no one asks what he means about that.

"It's time." Benton puts his pot back on, secures the chin strap. Gets to his knees, making to shoulder his weapon. "Who's with me?"

They are all ready to go down the draw into the desert town, silently, faces smudged and patterned. To take out the insurgent cell they know hides in plain sight. And for some pay back. A lot of pay back.

They tell me to stay up in this draw with the radio, along with Willie. And Benton says, "You stay here Birdman, if you know what's good. You wanna see your mama again. And Ese. We never left you. You never say otherwise, dig?"

There is a river of cold rushing down my chest and into my arms, my legs, my heart. And a dark fog fills my head. We're supposed to watch these guys, not fuck with them. My vision is tunneled, and there is only one end to it. "Don't do this, B. Leave it. It can't end anyway good for you."

"You don't be worrying about me. You think about you!" He pulls his jacket sleeve free from my fingers. Slapping me on the helmet he ghosts into the dark.

I can't just let him go.

I tell WillieG the same before I go too. To stay here with the radio, and if he knows anything, it is that we all went into the town for close recon. Nothing else.

I have no plan, except not to lose Benton.

"Permian Basins!" He told me once over chow, his mouth spilling out bits of food and saliva in his excitement. "That's what I been reading about, you dig? These two bits of plate, you know, the planet's crust – one west of what would later be South America, one east of what would later be South Africa? But both those places were right together then man, all packed together! They both broke off their main plates and headed north, racing like mothers. One plate slams into the North American plate in what they call the Delaware Basin, and the other plate crashes – oh baby, I wish I could've been there to see – she slams into the Asian continent just about right where we are now!" He wipes his mouth with the back of his hand, not taking his eyes off me. "Can you believe it?!"

Nobody could get more excited about crazy shit like that than Benton. I just huffed a bit of laugh, shaking my head, a folded piece of bread I was using to mop up gravy waving vaguely around in the air over my plate.

"So, there's all this life in a shallow sea! Just one sea, covering everything, surrounding just one continent. Pangea! Hundreds of millions of years! Millions of living species, swarming, all the time, all kinds of things! Billions of life cycles – mitotic division? – growing, dying, settling. Always settling! Fuck me!"

I don't know where he gets all this. He reads a lot. Makes me wonder what he's gonna do when he gets home. Makes me wonder what else he knows. I can't picture him anywhere but here.

When I get down to the town the rebels are all gone, a lot of them blown away, along with a good bit of the rest of the place. And Benton too. And T-Bone and the others. All gone. I feel cold. Lost. My legs don't hold me up.

I heard the firefight, like its own tiny war, as I ran stumbling down, too late. I should've gone with him. I should've knocked him out. Goddamnit Benton. Fuck it, I say. I lay down my rifle, put my arm under his head. Close his eyes. My heart feels like lead. I don't want to, but I can't help it. I feel tears on my cheek.

I get back hours later, use the radio to call it in. It's still there, but WillieG is nowhere around. I go looking for him, waiting for the different shitstorm that'll come down from above for all this. Benton, you asshole.

● ● ●

Later I dream I am searching through the records of men who died in service to their country, and I find this entry:

Charles Artemis Bird, bronze star, Vietnam, 1970

In the dream it is me, but I don't have any problem with that. It makes sense to me. It feels like in the dream I am already dead. In the dream though, I know when I wake up I will be covered in sand, and not yet dead. While I am in the dream, there is a point, a continuation of existence only punctuated by death.

So I had fought and died in Vietnam. And who knows how many wars before that. So what if that was true, and it was only for now that I was fighting in a desert? Wasn't there a movie about a famous soldier who thought that? That he lived only to fight in war?

It feels a little bit like that for me. Vietnam. Iraq. Afghanistan. Except I think I remember that in the movie the guy really loved what he was doing.

15

CMC - San Luis Obispo
_/_/2007. The Present.

The officers at the prison are so used to me now that their visitor intake procedures for me are no more than perfunctory. Makes me wonder if smuggling something in could be that easy - just visit a lot?

I am waved along to the usual visiting room. When he comes in, he does not look unhappy to see me. Hard to tell with him. But he sits right down at the table with me, a question barely shrouded in his eyes.

"Names, Mr. Ray. I need names."

"Just Ray is good."

"Ray? You want me to address you as 'Ray'?"

"It's good." Is all he says.

"Ray, then. I need names of men you remember from your old platoon." His mouth starts to open and I barge in, "I know you don't want to play - but I need this. You said it would be fair. Can you please try?"

He actually smiles at me.

"What."

"You sure you ain't part black?" He smiles some more. But the question in him has faded.

My mouth is open, again. His shoulders move in a kind of silent chuckle.

"I saw Captain Inaugieu."

The smile is wiped off his face. But it is not replaced with anything.

"I spoke with him".

"What did he say?"

I watch him.

"I also spoke to Skinny Planchett."

Now his face really is blank.

"You don't know him? Never heard of him?"

"It's possible. Was he in 'Nam?"

I nod.

"I hardly remember any of that. One of the reasons I don't want to talk about it."

"Said he knew you. Back when. Thought you got a pretty shitty deal."

"Did he."

"So do I."

"How would you know? Why do you care?"

I can't say any thing to him about that. We watch each other. The tectonic plate on which we ride moves a fraction of an inch. Something shifts.

"There was a kid I met once while we were both in the stockade, in California. A kid then, anyway."

"That's good, Ray. I need names from Vietnam though."

"A white boy. Quiet. Brought me chow one evening, stayed outside the door. I asked him what he wanted."

"'Nothing,' he said. 'Are you the guy they're framing for what happened in Vietnam? Those two officers?'"

"Who was he?" I ask.

"Don't interrupt. I tell him to fuck off. He didn't go right away.

"Then he says, 'Ok, sorry. It's none of my business.' And he still doesn't go. I could feel him out there, waiting. 'Only?' this kid says, 'Stay strong. We know about you. I mean, this is important and it's fucked up what they're doing. To you. So. Don't give up?'

"'Fuck you.' I tell him. 'Don't give up.' I mock him. 'Shit,' I say. 'What do you know about it. About anything. White boy. I told you to fuck off,' I spit out. And then he goes. Goddam liberal pissant white boy." And Ray looks up pointedly at me, like he is looking over some glasses.

"It's alright," I tell his eyes. "Call me whatever you want. Tell me to fuck off. Not saying I will, but you can say anything to me."

"Yeah. Well. There I am, feeling totally on my own. Lawyer's alright. But I am in the white man's cage. And we all know how this shit ends." He looks at me again.

I nod.

"So, another time I'm just getting dropped back in the can after a visit from the lawyer, and this kid is standing outside my cell and he's got a mop and a bucket and kind of cart. He's in fatigues, but he's got stripes on his arm. Three of them. And he watches while the two MPs shove him to one side and get me into my cell and lock the door. It's all unnecessary, man. I am not going anywhere. I could see he was furious about being treated like that by the Man, but all he gives back, to me, is this weak smile. Outside I can hear the Mips ask the kid what he's doing there. He tells them he's the janitor, just doing his job. They mock him pretty good and take their boots on down the hall. I can hear them laughing to each other."

Ray isn't looking right at me, but I feel like he is waiting for something, from me.

"So?" I prompt. He gives the smallest twitch, like I had interrupted him somewhere, alone with his thoughts.

"So?" He glares at me and returns to this story.

"'A janitor? With three stripes?' I give him, and he says, 'It's all I'm willing to do in here.'

"And I say, 'In here? You mean like In Here? What'd you do?' And he says, 'Refused orders to go to Vietnam.' And I can't help a snort at that. I laugh at him too. 'Shit. Boy, they gonna shoot your white ass.' And he comes right back and says, 'Not shoot. It's not desertion under fire. Put me away though. Maybe 25 years.' And that stops me.

"'What are they waiting for then?' I pick up and go after him. I couldn't help myself. The way he said it? Like he was ready for it? Like, maybe he's already there, even."

"Like you were already there?" I guess out loud.

I can read no answer to that in his face. He just goes on. "He tells me, 'They have to do a court martial. You know about that.'"

Ray pushes his face just that little bit closer to mine, looking in that moment maybe 25 years younger, and says to me, "And I tell the kid, 'I know about that. Yeah, I do,'"

He settles back into his chair and I watch him suddenly grow back all of his age, and maybe some extra, his eyes down at his hands. "I surely do."

He stays like that a long time, and I am thinking he may want me to go right now. I sit forward and start just a bit to scoot my chair back from the table. He looks right up and says, "The kid, that white sergeant, tells me he's gotta get back to work and gives his bucket and cart both a shove I can hear, and I say, 'Wait.' And he stops. And I say, 'Why do you do this?' And I do not know why I am asking a white man why he is doing anything. What the fuck difference does it make, I think.

"And he says, 'See, I'd brought my fatigues back with me when I turned myself in. I had this idea, me getting checked in, them taking my civvies, cutting my hair. Then what? Giving me what to wear? Did stockade prisoners wear special uniforms? So I had my stuff in a duffel I'd brought in. I'm wearing them now and when I first came in, I was standing out by the wire facing into the deeper parts of the base, looking at the California winter sky above the fence. It was just settling in on me. I was in, they could do pretty much anything they wanted with me. I had a case, but not a hope. I started to see that I could stay like this, never see anyone again. Never know freedom. And I thought, it was all out there now. Everything I could want. Everyone I love. Even my fight. That was out there too. I'm in here. And that fence is the line.

'I could've said I wanted to die, but that wasn't true. I just wanted not to hurt. And having everything out there and nothing in here, that hurt really bad. So I started in right then, on letting everything go. I told myself, 'This is my world now. There is nothing out there for me. What I have is this stretch of gravel, this wire, these low buildings behind me. And this empty sky."

"And the kid stands like that looking up at the ceiling, like he could see a sky through it, and I thought he was done. But he's not. 'Then a bird flew in low, across the sky, above the fence.' he says, 'I don't know what kind. It didn't matter. And it made a cry. I don't remember what kind. But it cut into me, ripped me open. And I spilled onto the gravel, my insides at my feet, my heart tearing free to leap up at the bird. Everything I ever wanted, flying free, away from me.'"

Ray breathes, leans back, eyes up. Like maybe he can see something past the ceiling.

Then he leans in, nods his head up and down a couple times, "That was some crazy shit."

"How do you remember all that?" I can't help asking.

"That? I do not know. I didn't know I did. Maybe I got it all wrong. Sometimes I think I made up the kid. I was bad crazy myself at the time." His eyes touch mine.

I am starting to feel like this is his way of testing me. I nod once, pull my lips together.

As I get up to go he asks, "What about that 'visit' you made to the deserts of Iraq?"

I almost forget I'd told him. I have trouble remembering what happened when, or where. But he no sooner asks me than he launches into this very strange 'sermon' kind of thing, doing full-on 'Preacher Man' – eyes to heaven, arms wide out.

"'And a river flowed out of Eden, watering the Garden.'"

He looks at me, gauging my mood, my response, and with a normal voice adds, "At least that's what it says in Genesis."

Talk of the Bible makes me anxious. And from Ray, like this? I hold my breath.

With a small nod of his head and an arm pointing now to the door, he continues. "'So they were driven out, out of the East gate, and to the East they went.'" He drops his arm, lowers his head a little and if possible his face becomes even more serious. "'And Uriel,' he thunders, 'stood at the East Gate with his flaming sword that turned *every* way.'" With a sudden mischievous grin, and bringing his two hands together in a smart single clap, clasped hands continuing to rise toward the ceiling, as his eyes look up to follow them, he intones, dropping to his lowest register on the last word, 'And Eden was ... Lost.'"

I find my mouth open and close it quickly. "What are you on about Ray? Eden? Lost?" I feel a shiver rising in me, perhaps in answer to my own questions. "The only Eden I know was the one in the James Dean movie."

No. That's not true. My mother read the Bible to me. Genesis. The floor trembles under the soles of my shoes. Pangaea. In motion again.

As if he's reading me, inside me, the thinnest smile appears on his lips with the smallest shake of his head. His great dark eyes holding mine.

"'The Eastern Gate is named Basra.'" He pauses. I narrow my eyes. "'And since the casting out, the river flowing from its mouth has been a river of life. A river of sorrow.'"

I know this story, the gist of it anyway. Eden lost. All of us aching to return. I knew, or thought I knew, what the ache was supposed to be about.

I say, "Amongst all the things that might have been, and are no more, was idyllic and eternal life. That's how it goes, right?"

He claps me on the knee. Then his eyes let me go, his vision lengthens in the silence of the room and he seems somehow to leave it.

To where?

When he comes back he brings something different. "Maybe Steinbeck had it figured," he says conversationally, as if there had been no pause. "He wrote that book, that your movie came from? East of Eden. He says, '... every civilization teaches that a man who kills must be destroyed. ... And then we take a soldier and put murder in his hands and tell him, Use it wisely.'

"I think about what Steinbeck called 'the secret pond ... where evil and ugly things germinate and grow strong' but are somehow held there."

Steinbeck?

"Except? I heard of a guy, went to the desert. Trained shooter. After months of no action, one night he sees in his sights what he thinks is an unarmed man. But he IDs the guy from the shoot-on-sight list. A very bad man. He hesitates, concerned about rules of engagement and about his own feelings. Shooting an unarmed man. He misses the opportunity.

"The thing is, after his tour, he can't let go of why. Why did he let that target go. Afraid to kill?

Afraid to make a mistake in such a great matter? Simple lack of guts?

"I think he is still thinking about what he missed. Trained to kill, steeped in motivation about right and wrong in global conflict, about killing the enemy. I think he no longer believes it is wrong to kill, just wrong to kill for the wrong reasons. I think he is wishing for an opportunity to have the right reasons. The right enemy."

The 'right enemy'. It's a thought I haven't been able to get out of my own head.

"Like Steinbeck, I am sure that 'the dark pools in some men grow an evil strong enough to wriggle free'".

And with that he is up, and walking to the door. He turns to me. "And I am one of those men."

He does not say that he thinks I am one too. But that is what I read in his eyes.

He taps the door once, his escort appears and Ray leaves with him. Not a word or glance at me.

I stay, still seated, orbiting Ray's dark thoughts, still swirling in the room he's just left. I wonder, if my mother had read that book, if she'd also thought about what Steinbeck had said, as she read me the passages of Genesis. I wonder if she'd kept hidden from me, and the rest of us, a yearning of her own, for this lost Eden.

It's a good place to sit with this question. This space that is itself so cut off from all that humans could hope for. I take that with me back to my room.

• • •

When I was 19, I thought I missed my mother. But I realize now that it was only something I'd just never been without. Like a limb. Or my appetite.

Still, the ache so pervasive I did not fully realize it until so many years had passed that I had forgotten what it was like to have a mother.

16

There is nothing quite so dark as night in the desert. Perhaps there are darker places. The bottoms of caves, trenches in the oceans, alone at night with the lights off in a dark room with the covers pulled up overhead, shivering, waiting for ... it ... to reveal itself. But dark in the desert with no moon is a different kind of dark. Very different.

For one thing, there is just enough light from the stars to allow for the possibility, the faintest possibility, of a moving shadow. And not enough absolute blackness to sharpen hearing and smell, or proximity, or any other senses secondary in humans to sight. A moving shadow, yes.

The shadow is moving, faintly, erratically. Not enough to be caught as – something – in anyone's peripheral vision. But something. Someone?

It flows like the ever-tumbling winds across the erg. Eyes and face hooded, hands gloved, or darkened.

A moment's work to scoop out a hollow in front of the small tent's entrance, to bury the small explosive device with its compression trigger, and be gone. Like a passing swirl of sand.

Iraq. Al Anbar Province.
_/_/2007. The Present.

It wasn't hard to find where Blake had stashed the rug this time. If anything, he was getting more careless. Maybe he'd started thinking about the bad luck too. Maybe he wanted it to be found, confiscated, out of his life. I wondered if that had something to do with the way he'd desecrated it, trying to tame it, control it. Kill it. Sonofabitch.

I found it under a pile of tools in one of the houses we'd commandeered after our first recon here. I had to move some of the tools, and then it slid out fairly quickly. He had it wrapped in a tarp and tied with bungee cord. Even through the wrap I could smell the rankness of their beer and urine, my anger flaring again. Rotten bastards.

I waited at the door to be pretty sure no one was watching and I ran across the alley with it under my arm, and along a bullet-pocked stucco wall toward the edge of the village where I threw it down behind a pile of rubble and kicked a bunch of it over the tarp to half-way disguise it until I could come back for it at night.

Not that night, as it turned out, because the CO had sent the whole platoon out on a night op, a sweep up the wadis surrounding the village to find and destroy any incursionary lurkers out there. Usually there's nobody out there, but the Gunny says it discourages them to know we'll be out after them. Still. We always go fully keyed up. One little goof, and sure as hell that's the night they find us, instead of the other way around. This night was same-ol-same-ol though, and we all came back with that left over combat jitter. That tingling in my arms, my legs, my gut. That rancid taste in the back of the throat. At least that's how it was for me.

Always makes me mad, like I want to fight. I picture Blake's face, then Rivers. No way to go up against them directly, even if I had the balls for it. They'd stick together, the whole rotten bunch of them. And one of them would get me. And I didn't come out here to die at the hands of scum like that. Or to get arrested. There was that, even if I didn't die.

No. And it came to me then, like the fellow says, 'So many ways to get dead. In the desert.' And I almost couldn't believe what I was thinking, even as my thoughts raced ahead, planning it, rough planning it, all the way out. Blake and Rivers, bivvied up, stealthy night intruder, IED. The whole thing. I couldn't erase those thoughts from my head, I couldn't scrub them out. I was ashamed. And still, part of me wouldn't let go. An evil part. I told myself right then I would never do that, not even to lice like them. Never.

But they wouldn't hesitate to do that to me. Maybe not with an IED. But we also had a saying, 'If anybody wants you dead out here, you're dead.' And as soon as they couldn't find the rug, they'd know who took it. Even if I hadn't, they'd still come for me. They were gonna go right for me. That was a fact. And they would enjoy it.

So. They weren't really Marines. They were a disgrace to the Corps. And they wanted me dead. That made them the Enemy, and this was war.

At the end of the next day, after our second patrol through the village, and after chow, I went out to the edge of town and sat for awhile watching the sun go down. Not very smart, sitting alone like that, but I didn't want a partner in on this with me.

I watched the afternoon wind dying, kicking up devils of sand and then just letting them drop. Kind of like us out here. Kicking hell out of the rebels, then just pulling out, letting it all drop. The wind had been doing this forever, with all the time in the world to shape the face of this desert. We didn't have that. Time. When we were gone, gone for good? There wouldn't be a trace of any of us left. Not the bad. Not the good either. Maybe a memory, stored in the hearts of a family that had lost kin to an invader and went on with their lives, like they'd always done. Only this time, if I were true, they'd get back a little something shouldn't have been taken at all.

When the sun went down, I walked over to the half buried tarp, pulled it free, and walked into the sand.

17

Iraq 2007 - Vietnam 1970

He put one foot in front of the other. One sand-colored, steel-lined boot in front of the other. His eyes on the back of the man in front of him, and also restlessly, relentlessly on the ground in front of him and on the sandy horizon to either side. The Price of Freedom is Eternal Vigilance he'd read somewhere. The price of tomorrow in the desert was a different kind of vigilance, he was sure.

Where had his thoughts been a moment ago? Nothing vigilant about daydreaming, thinking about being back in the world? About water, and greenery? That kind of lapse could be fatal to his unit, not just to him, and he knew it. He doubled his attention as his squad leader called a halt and the Marines with him wordlessly took up a defensive rest formation. No one said anything about digging in, so he settled his pack and his armor straps to just a bit more wearable position, checked his gear, inspected his weapon and cautiously opened his canteen.

'What are you doing here Charlie?' He asked himself. 'Are you dreaming? Jesus!'

His reinforced Company was nowhere. Not nowhere on the map, just Nowhere. As in nothing to see. But that didn't mean there was nothing out there. They had come this way to find what was out here, besides sand. And they always did (he knew that, but how?). He unstrapped his helmet briefly to lift it, clear his brow, resettle it and button up again. He took three small and slow swigs of water, his eyes moving constantly.

• • •

"Birdman!" He heard his name called. The sand vanished. Replaced instantly by so much green he felt suddenly tied up in it.

"Sergeant?" he replied, standing to face Hess the platoon sergeant, and then almost falling in a wave of dizziness.

"I'm putting you with 3rd Platoon this afternoon. I know you haven't had your rest and last night was rough. Are you up to it?"

Charlie knew he was being ordered, not asked. But Hess' concern seemed genuine. "Sure," he said.

"Could be another hot one today, Birdman. You're the best. More important, with Swindle down, you're all 3rd's got. Make me proud."

Charlie stifled a yawn, stretched his stiff muscles, felt the glue of stale sweat that held his outfit to his skin. "Will do." He went to pickup up his medical pack and check it for resupply from Company stores.

In the medical stores locker, he quickly found extra bandage, morphine, sterile dressings, and battlefield stitching. He held the heavy thread in his hand and images of last night came back in a rush. Half a dozen men hit with mortar burst fragments, and the rest of the platoon good and pinned down. He not only had his own hands full, he was giving orders to everybody near by – hold pressure here, hold him still, get that package out of my pack, cover this one up, hold his head, Now goddam it! Four of those guys were going home today, but none of them in a bag.

I hate this, he thought. Except for the lucky ones with the stateside

tickets home, he was sewing guys up
so they could go out and get blown
up again. Fucking Army.

San Luis Obispo
_/_/2007. The Present.

It's like I'm standing in a place where two streams come together and make eddies in the current. But before they're mixed, they are distinct and separate and simultaneous, and I can smell both streams.

But these are not streams of water.

The two streams that I'm feeling today are the present here with Ray – and maybe with Rena – and also a stream from my younger days in Estacado County with Eileen. The sun shining down now on an iconic California beach and the sun shining on the red dirt of a warm afternoon at the ranch outside of Babylon 50 years ago. I can feel both streams moving past me and I am in both of them at the same time. That makes them the same time, for me.

Last night I found I could stand in a dream and be awake at the same time, one slowly fading into the other.

• • •

Ray's got me thinking about this 'river of sorrow' of his. About rivers from high valleys. 'Gardens,' I guess you could call them. And about centuries of warfare. Surely there were wars all over the globe, and maybe some of them had nothing to do with rivers? But the two I know best about, I feel like I have first hand experience with, both are interwoven with the course of such rivers. The Tigris Euphrates and the Mekong.

I read up about the Mekong long ago. Mother of Waters it is called in some native dialects. Rises from streams in the northern Himalayas, pours out and down from a basin that some would say was a garden, of sorts. Pristine, untrammeled by the muck of civilization of any kind. A region from which some history also says a people came, or perhaps were ejected, to move southward into Indochina ten thousand years ago.

I have heard it said that the two rivers in Iraq, or maybe more precisely, the mountainous regions from which they flow, are also called mother of waters, or something like that. Coincidence? Whimsy on my part? All I know is that people have been killing each other along or near the source of both of those river systems for most of the last several thousand years. And what about that? Can't that be related to the whole 'lost Eden' thing? We all yearn so for peace, a land of peace and plenty, that we are willing to kill for it?

Or maybe it's not all of us. Maybe the 'gardens' of the world are valuable in a much more practical, exploitable way. And so maybe it is not the many, but the few who would fight for domination of such resources, who would call for war. And then, for the thousands of reasons, or no reasons at all, that young men have always been willing, even eager, to fight – to prove themselves, to vindicate a cause, or just to kill – then those few would have an army. An army to take what they wanted, and call it anything but what they were doing. And dress it, coat it, with the noble

Isms that stir our human hearts, while betraying all such humans, and their hearts.

Two rivers of sorrow, that I know of. And one great river of greed.

18

US Army Criminal Investigation Command
Quantico, Virginia
_/_/2007. The Present.

Tuyet never asked me to prove anything. She asked me to find Ray, to make a bridge. Bring her grandfathers together. I guess I am on my way to that. What we'd do with that? That was another matter. The proving is just for me.

I knew if I was going to continue with the proving, stuck as I appeared to be, that I ought to get help. A real detective, not a burned-out vet and part-time fact jockey like me. It occurred to me that I might be able to find out something from the Army's own investigation, however biased it might have been. And with the two murders still unsolved all these years, maybe there was some kind of cold case unit in the Army I could go to.
I did some checking and found that the whole 'cold case' phenomenon was relatively recent, only maybe 15-20 years back or so. Nothing like that at the end of the war in Vietnam. In fact, I learned that the first big upswing in cold case interest and investigation was born of advances in DNA and other forensic sciences at the end of the century, and that

it had been picked up in a big way in 1995 by Naval Criminal Investigative Service, so called NCIS.

Then I dug a little further and found that the Army, not to be outdone, created their own 'Cold Case' Unit inside Army Criminal Investigation Command just before the millennium. That's where I needed to go. And that's where I went, by some round-about ways and plenty of bureaucratic crapola. And I found this old lifer, a warrant officer, who was willing to talk to me.

"Listen Bud ... any detective would've started right off to find out who did do it ... not try to prove your friend didn't." He wasn't being rude to me, but he didn't seem much interested either. A little condescending, I guess.

"But in this case, any of these cases, 2000 of them in Vietnam in 1969, 70 and 71, by some accounts, there was never going to be any way to find out who did it. Or even which side did it."

I told him, "I read that. The Army has thousands of these cases, unsolved fraggings. That they've officially denied all but two of them. The rest they blame on 'enemy action'."

"Yeah. And one of the two they do acknowledge features your friend Clayton Ray. Only in their book, that case is not cold, it's closed."

So I asked him to help me find the names that Ray did give me after all. Ray had said he wasn't sure anymore, wished me good luck finding any of them. Marashal. And Petty. As for good luck?

San Diego
_/_/2007. The Present.

"Yeah, he was with us that night," Joe Marashal tells me. "At least the part I can remember." He laughs at the memory. "We were all seriously wasted on some Thai stick Petty had scored. If he left, I never noticed!"

Petty tells me the same thing, pretty much. "He was laughing and cutting up about blowing up somebody's shit – like, wouldn't it be a gas if we'd do that? Of course we all thought it was just the weed talking – which somehow only made it funnier. You know? Jeez, what a bunch of crazy fuck-ups we were." When I ask him if he noticed Ray leaving, even to pee, he says, "I wouldn't have noticed if my own dick was on fire!"

I ran into both of these guys in San Diego at a dog track. They looked like hell. Maybe they thought the same of me. I never knew either of them of course, but since we'd been in the same camp the night of the killing, and Ray gave me their names, I looked for them. I was hoping they could be more positive, despite the slant that Captain Inaugieu had put on them all as a lying bunch of losers. From what I could tell, the loser part was true, or was by this time. But who am I to have an opinion about that. I haven't made much of my own life.

I asked them if they remembered any of the others. They gave me a couple other names, pretty much matched what Ray remembered. But they had no idea where I could find them, if any of them were still alive. I asked my guy about it and he had the names run through NCIC, got one hit. Hillis Rawlins was serving time on drug charges in Herlong, north of Reno. I got permission to visit.

FCI Herlong, NV
_/_/2007. The Present.

"Ray and me was tight," he tells me. He doesn't volunteer anything else.

"Do you remember the explosion? The one they said Ray did? Killed the two officers?"

"I don't remember shit from that night, man. I don't remember shit from the whole time I was over there. I stayed high all the time." He looks at me. I could believe him on the memory part. He doesn't look like he even knows where he is now. "But I heard about the dead white boys. Shee-it! That must've been something!" He laughs.

"But Ray was with you that night, right?"

"I don't know where Ray was, man – I told you, I don't know where I was!"

"Ray told me he was with you and Petty and Marashal and a couple others that night," I prompt him.

"Ray told me he did it. I was proud of the brother."

"He told you that? When?"

"Before they arrested him. Said he tied a grenade on the CO's door and laughed his ass off."

"But it wasn't the CO's door. It was some other officers."

"All the same to me man."

"Was it all the same to Ray?" I ask, really pissed off now at this guy.

"Huh. Like he give a shit."

"Are you saying Ray told you he did it and didn't care who died?" I want to grab this fucker and drag him through the wire.

"No. I'm saying Ray told me he did it and he said he laughed about it. He was all, I don't know, disappointed or something when it turns out it wasn't the Captain."

I didn't know what to think, or say. I'd come here to gather more evidence of Ray's innocence. Not this drug addled condemnation. "You got it in for Ray?"

"Me? No. Ray's my man. I look up to the brother." He comes on so simple, it looks like maybe he believes what he's telling me. "He doing all right?"

"Yeah," I tell him. "He's doing his time."

CMC - San Luis Obispo
_/_/2007. The Present.

After that, I drove all night back to San Luis Obispo, couldn't get my mind onto anything else. Not one person to stand there and tell me they were with Ray, knew he didn't do it. And now another one who was sure, even glad, that he had? True, both 'witnesses' were badly flawed. Maybe I was just too far out on thin ice. Maybe I needed new meds.

But I knew Ray hadn't done the murders – so what was all this I was feeling? Anger, betrayal, stupidity. And of course more anger.

I got my usual room out by the prison, or one so close I couldn't tell the difference. Slept a few hours, restlessly, cleaned up and went to the prison without eating first.

As soon as Ray comes in, this time actually looking glad to see me, I let all that anger hit him.

"*Did* you do those two lieutenants?"

He stops dead just inside the door, and it slowly closes on its own behind him. One hand has started on its way in my direction and dies in mid-air. Frozen for the moment. I watch his old face collapse layer by layer. Then all his limbs seem to go limp, and I relent and move a chair up to catch him.

"Ray. I'm sorry, man. I'm a little crazy, and way short on sleep." I go for the other chair.

His head is down on his chest. I feel terrible. What was I thinking? Still the bull in the damn china shop.

"Ray, I'm sorry. Let's start over. I *know* you didn't kill those men! But you have no idea what people have been saying to me!"

"Sure I do." The words come up from his chest as if they had bypassed his head. He raises his chin just an inch off his chest. "I told you. Everyone believes I killed them. That's what you heard." He looks up at me now. "I just did not expect to hear it from you. Not now. Before, maybe."

In a further thoughtless gesture, I reach across and take hold of the back of his arm. What I felt then was ... like being outside of something I have felt inside, all my life. The liquid boiling volcanic rage, isolating, cutting off, shielding and swelling for violent action. I drop my hand, sit back quickly. Distance. Immediate distance. It's what I would want.

He straightens up. "No matter," he says. "It's bound to happen, to keep coming up. "There's nothing I can tell you though. I didn't ask you to look into this. I told you I was tired of it. Tired to death."

I let it go. He is right. I don't know what to do next. Without much looking at each other, we both let time, and the fumes of his anger, pass.

"Do you ever think about them," I ask.

"Yeah. I think about them."

Inaugieu told me the parents of the two dead officers had written back to him, thanking this predator for his kindness. Asking what he could do to bring the killer to justice. He didn't say exactly but it was apparent that he had done more than just write the official Army condolence letters. That he had separately, and unofficially, written them with his own conclusions. About Ray.

"Not at first," Ray continues. "And then not for a long time."

I sit in his silence. Sometimes it seems our meetings are mostly silence.

He looks up at me, tracks my eyes.

"You know that bastard sent the wife the fragments of a letter that one of them had been writing the night he died?"

"I don't know that, but I was guessing something like that, from the way he acted when I talked to him."

"There was just the explosion you know. No fire. Lots of stuff got shredded, or vaporized. But nothing burned." His deep brown eyes are distant, and rearward. Tunnels to another time. "And then she sent that letter to me."

My thoughts go in a hundred directions, I can't track any of them. Then I notice he is looking at me. Here, now. And those eyes are merry.

"S'matter Homes," he goes ebonic on me, "new development in yo' case?"

I feel some kind of relief, and it comes out of me as two puffs of a weak chuckle. "No. I mean yes. But ... What? What case? There is no 'case', and if there was it's not mine."

"Mine then?" he offers.

It's my turn for silence. I watch him for a long moment. There is an openness I haven't noticed before. A lack of hostility. "It's always been yours, hasn't it." I offer, watching him. "And now you tell me this? How long?"

"Since I got that bit of letter? Almost 30 years." He smiles. It is not the right kind of smile. "Like I said, I didn't think much about it, not then. They were nothing to me. Two more white guys added to the pile."

He seems to be looking backward again. "I was still very angry," he says, but maybe not to me. He still has that misplaced smile, but I can see his eyes back there, somewhere. "Made some kind of impression on me though. Never forgot." He comes back to me then, distance and smile gone from his face. Left behind. "You know?"

Yes I know. Not about his thing though. About my thing. Things. Never far from me. Never forgotten. Yes.

I must've nodded at him. He goes on. "There were three of them. That night." He looks a question at me that I can not read. "There were three of them. Two second louies, cherries, coming in as platoon leaders, and one more, the one that survived, just passing through." He is going distant again, even as he speaks, eyes, even voice, receding.

I had heard from returning officers about the heat and humidity.
And I thought I knew what to expect.

Ray's voice is not only distant, it is a different voice, a different accent.

"That's the first lines of the letter," he says in his own voice. "Make's him sound like a sweet guy. It gets worse. Listen."

The different voice again.

It could not be much worse than the summer I spent on the coast of Georgia, could it? Remember that? Well, yes, it can. It hit me like the proverbial wet blanket when I stepped off the plane in Cam Ranh Bay. A very steamy, nastily invasive blanket. Not content to lie on me and cover me, it immediately insinuated itself beneath my uniform, into my underwear, my skin. Like something hungry and alive and inexorable.

Ray pauses in his recollection, as if he's flipping pages. Opening old boxes. Who knew what his memory looked like. "You remember that Bird? How it was always hungry?"

"Yes." I nod once.

"He put in some more stuff about smelling spilled jet fuel, hot asphalt, hot metal. How that was some kind of background for the smell of what he called 'a hot, living, breathing thing'."

Something that was here before us,
and will be here when we are gone.

The fingers of Ray's two hands work themselves together, weaving, sliding past one another and back again. Back and forth.

"You think about that Bird? 'Here before us'? And there when we are gone?"

I do. A lot. But I don't say anything about it.

He lapses back into his reverie then, in the voice I now think of as that long-dead, young officer.

Tonight, I've laid out the few
things I need around me in my new
quarters – my hooch they call it – the
few things I need, to remind me of
you.

I see Ray's mouth working then, but no sound coming out. A small spasm flies quickly across his face, just under his eyes. And he goes on.

It's very Spartan here, all
completely squared away, and I am
sure I will get used to it very soon. I
have two other roommates, both
officers, one of them new here like me,
and as you might expect, very anxious
not to let it show how very
uncomfortable the whole jungle thing
is for him. Me too, but I don't mind
telling you. You'd figure me out in a
minute!

As Ray resurrects this ghost, my own reptile brain has been going on full alert. My breathing has become rapid and shallow. The back of my neck is cold and damp. But it is also a little like a trance for me too. Then I notice he has stopped and I look up at him. He's very present – I sense his own alertness – but his face is a complete blank. It startles me.

Ray asks me, "Isn't it … scary? How the words are exact? They never change."

I just look at him. It's him that's scary.

He continues then, without any more stops, like he's in the last mile of a marathon, all systems exhausted, running on fumes, on the memory of endurance.

Things are pretty quiet here now, and I expect I will unroll my net and strip to my skivvies and climb in under and try my first night's sleep in this alien place. Tomorrow I have to look my best for the CO and the men I will meet in my platoon. I said it was quiet, and I mean the sounds of the Army. But it is not quiet of all sounds. The night air buzzes with the wings of what I can only imagine are thousands of insects, maybe millions, and the exotic cries of birds on the hunt that I may never get a good look at. And then there are all the clicks and pops punctuating the humming and buzzing. I have no idea what they are made by, though some of them sound almost metallic. Here, there's someone outside at the screen of our door, I think. I'll go check then I'll come back and say goodnight.

We both sit a long time, no one speaks. The presence of the long dead letter writer, like a living thing now, a dreaded thing, in the room with us.

'Goodnight,' the young man had written. Goodnight. We could all say goodnight, that last goodnight. Ray sits emptied. No expression on his face, his body slack, those weaving fingers now quiet. A thin sliver shining on the bottom rim of his left eye.

"Goodnight," I say to him. And get up and leave.

19

San Luis Obispo
_/_/2007. The Present.

That night, alone and sick in my room, I had a dream. Another one. I hope it was a dream. Or had I left … gone to be with that Marine. I can't really tell anymore.

> *There were only three of us, and a dozen or more of them in there.*
> *We thought.*
> *We had to go in quick, miss nothing and keep surprise on our side. Somehow, I went in first and left the others behind. I shot everyone I met, no one escaped unharmed.*
> *Hospital patients. Nurses. Doctors.*
> *No armed insurgents. I couldn't stop. Didn't want to. Didn't wonder. At first. Missed no one.*
> *Gradually, I began to wonder about being selective, passed up first one, then another. Then stopped.*
> *Frozen.*

The full weight of horror,
agony crashed over me.
My mates slammed in behind
me. Stopped. Shock and sickened
wonder on their faces as they took in
what I'd done. I could not look away.
The faces so different from mine, the
faces of those I'd shot showing only
their own surprise and wonder.

How had I become what I
loathed? How had it been almost
casual, routine? How did I not
realize what I was doing and turn
my weapon upon myself?

Vietnam
1970.

It is the fear of some of us that our comrades in arms will turn to do us harm, sometimes capriciously. Other times with malice. For some real or imagined slight. Or in response to their own guilty fear that nothing less than taking us out will provide a safe path for their continued existence.

We all had that fear, everywhere I looked. Which was strange, in a way, because we fought and sweated along side each other, and few of us doubted the courage of our fellows, or that they would jump and risk their lives to save us. And still, this nagging sense that caprice, or malice, could and perhaps would rear its head without warning and shut off our dreams.

So we kept our weapons clean, if we could, a round chambered, safety on, pointed down range – and ever ready to bring it around if …

"Charlie, you ever think about what you left," Grease asks me one night after chow. "You know. What's waiting for you back in the world?"

Grease doesn't talk much, ever. It makes him a good shoulder buddy. For me anyway. I have a lot on my mind and I hate chatter. He's the only one in the unit doesn't call me 'Doc'. "No." I say, inviting no further discussion.

"Com'on Charlie, you know what I mean. I won't tell if that's what you're worried about."

I'm curious what's gotten into him. "S'matter Grease? Suck something bad up your butt and now you got diarrhea coming out the other end?"

"What?" That stops him, but most likely because the plumbing metaphor I've just rung has gone right past him. Then he goes on, "Doc you say the goddamnedest things. 'Scuse the fuck outta me for asking." And he makes to go off by himself. Which is what I wanted, but I feel bad anyway.

"What's eating you, Grease?"

He looks at me. Makes a business of rummaging in his jacket pocket for his smokes, finally shaking out a crumpled and disreputable cig and getting it lit. "I do." He says, exhaling."Think about what I left home." He studies his boots. "I'm starting to do it a lot. It's got me worried. Like it's bad luck, or something."

"What do you think of?"

"Nothing in particular. I mean not the same thing always. Sometimes just a place I used to go with my buddies, drink beer, shoot pool, get in trouble. You know."

"What else? A girl?"

He looks far away for a long time. "Nah. Not a girl. Women, yes. But not a special girl." He finishes his smoke, field strips it. "I don't know if that's ever gonna be for me. You know?" He looks up at me with a smile so shy and unaffected, I could almost have loved the guy.

"So what's wrong with all that?"

"Nothing. But doesn't it worry you? When you think like that?"

It does. A lot. But I wasn't going to share that. "Not me. Like I said, I got a lot on my mind."

So, yeah, it could go like that. If it hadn't been in the middle of a jungle, I could be remembering it all fondly. Nice.

Later, days or weeks I don't remember, we were out on another night interdiction set up. Same ol' same ol'. Everybody was on edge of course. We all knew we could go from bored to heart-stopping fear in the space of a mosquito sting. The sun was going down. A screech from the bush split the air and a full auto burst sent rounds through the leaves just above my head and shattered a trunk 20 paces in front of me. I was in the dirt before the burst ended, and half the platoon was returning fire in all directions before any of us realized that the burst we'd heard was not from an AK-47.

It was one our own M16's. The firing stopped, amidst yells up and down the line, curses too. The only one not on the ground was Grease. He was standing, weapon up and over my head, finger still inside the guard, his face a frozen mask of horror. At what he had just done.

I left him standing like that and ran up the line to see if anyone had been hit. The Lieut was furious, the op ruined. He was running toward and then past me to maybe shoot Grease.

I only found one guy hurt – splinters from that shattered trunk in the back of his left arm.

And that's just about the worst of it, in many ways. Friendly fire, they say. Forget about it.

And then there is the murderous heart.

I was passing down the line, checking quinine rations, asking about toe rot, even handing out a few packages of penicillin ... nobody notices me when I am in Doc mode and there's no shooting or screaming. Two guys were talking low, heads together, but they did not stop as I went past, and what I thought I was hearing made me go slower ...

" ... maybe give'm a couple up the pipe next time the shit starts flying," one guy says.

"Shhh! You don't know who's listening," says his buddy.

"What? Out here? Fuck it. And fuck him. Let's just frag his ass. He's gonna die anyway, way he's going – the VC get him at night, or somebody else 'at hates him enough. We do it now, or soon, he doesn't take anybody else with him. And he doesn't shoot off his mouth anymore."

"You're crazy Geets, you know that?"

"No more'n you, Six. No more'n you. You think it's crazy, me knowing he's gonna rat us all out, sooner or later? Sooner, I figure. Corporal my-shit-don't-stink? We're doing all right here, you and me, right? We waste him, and keep up our collecting, we keep on keepin' on."

"Shhh! Jesus, Geets! – Hey Doc, you got anything for this shit behind my ear?" The guy we call Six Pack says, noticing me passing by.

"Yeah sure." I rummage in my kit, Geets looking at me scared. I do not meet his eye, but I hand Six Pack a couple packets of anti-fungal creme, looking at the side of his face. "Squeeze on half a packet now, then again before you sleep. Same tomorrow. Let me know how it works?"

He nods and looks away. The two of them shuffle their equipment around, pretending to be busy.

"Keep your heads down," I warn them, and move down the line.

• • •

I am lying in a bed. An impossibly white bed. And strung up with hoses and wires and hoists. Almost coming out of a fog, somewhere a radio playing something, Crosby, Stills and Nash I guess. Very familiar.

"... mother earth will swallow you ..." (like flies, musical flies, buzzing in my head, the voices in harmony call to me, calm me, ready me. It's where I have always wanted to be) "... buried in the ground." They sing. I slide. It's easy, now. I have fought and fought and it was so hard to do. This is the way I was meant to be. "... lay your body down."

Cost of freedom?

We were sliding across the muddy surface of a burned out field near a burned out village. The rain was so thick I thought we might breathe it in, grow fins, swim home. Sporadic rifle fire punctuated a rising chorus of incoming mortar explosions, and we had no cover, caught in the open. We had called in air support but nothing was coming in this rain. We also called coordinates for suppressing fire from the base, and the first shells were just landing across the stream along the line of trees from which we were seeing muzzle flashes.

I just wanted to go underground. But we couldn't just drop and start digging. Some of us would never be seen again.

A blast to my right sent its hot breath against my cheek as if the lukewarm rain was not even there. I saw two men drop and I stopped to crouch. I could not see them now. Damn. I half crawled, half hopped over to where I had seen them last. Nothing. Not a sign. God in all of his distant, far fucking away glory, help us.

Then a flash of light right in front of me.

In the darkness, I smell the fear in my own breath. And I cannot move a muscle.

20

San Luis Obispo
_/_/2007. The Present.

I wake up drenched. The bed sheets tangled around me. Where?

The universe, my universe is in this room with me. Constellations, galaxies. Deep planetary motion. Me in its tangled center, crushed. Broken by the weight of my own self-pity. 'Ahhhhh!' The cry escapes, my neck feels broken, my arms are cables for ripping down pyramids. The heat behind and above my eyes searing.

Then it has all just run out of me. The pills I find grasped in my left hand are forgotten.

I remember something else now, sometime after my body recovering ... recovering ... before all my returns to the VA half out of my head, before the intermittent twilight and fog of my existence on the street. I remember now returning to the ranch, in Babylon, in the early 70s, like I said I would never do. And forgotten ever since that I did.

I had left a home – that was not a home. I had crossed an ocean for a fight that was not mine. Fought and died, almost, in a land I feared, amongst a people I did not know. Except one. And her I left there.

Then, a long stay in a limbo of recuperation, self-pity and anger. But not home. Not the ranch. Not Babylon.

Charles Artemis Bird, itinerant snake oil salesman. And me my only customer.

'So what,' I would've said.

Well, first of all, the only oil I've ever really been involved with is the deep crude that lays hidden in the crust of the earth. And like a great lodestone, it has pulled me across time zones and national boundaries and years of feeling sorry for myself. To the place I started. Estacado County. The Great State of Texas. Eileen *had* found me.

I'd forgotten. She asked me to come down and work with her for a while.

"I'm profiled, Sugar. Can't do any heavy lifting." I'd told her. I did not want to admit, even to myself, how much I missed her, wanted to go down and just be with her.

"That's alright Charlie. You know the place, just could use some help with bossing the hands, things like that," she said. After a long pause, she added, "I miss you so much."

I think I mumbled something. Then rode a long train down to Babylon, or Odessa actually, and Eileen met me at the station. It was awkward for both us. A quick hug and a peck on my cheek, and some fumbled greetings and she drove me in the truck back to Babylon.

There was some small talk, gossip really, but nothing else all the way there. I was wishing I had just made up an excuse and told her 'No.' Every mile of the scenery filled me with a deeper dread, a kind of deadness I remembered too well from before I grabbed my pack and lit out, years ago.

When she pulled up to the main barn and shut off the engine, she turned herself in the seat to face me completely. "Look, I know this is going to start out bad for you. I know you just want to bolt and ... ." She looked at my eyes, tears welling up in hers, tossing her head like one of her mares and shaking it back and forth rapidly. "Goddamn it Charlie. I don't care if it is selfish! I just want you back. Here. With me." She put her head down then and her shoulders shook briefly.

I think my mouth was open, a little maybe, but I couldn't even think of words, much less say anything. I just wanted to throw my arms around her and hold her close. Maybe forever. But I couldn't.

"I swear Charlie, if you don't at least give this a try, here with me, and this goddamn pest-ridden ranch, I'll ... I'll take a pack and follow you to the ends of the earth. Fuck the damn place!"

Wasn't much I could say to that.

So, I did. Give it a chance. At least, I thought I was doing that. Then. Even now I tell myself I don't remember why it didn't last.

I put my head down and went to work, and not always with the medical team's blessings, I was pretty sure. I'd be really sore, and sometimes sick at night, and on a couple mornings I could not get out of bed. And Eileen would raise Cain and swear at me and threaten to kill me herself if I would not take better care. And after a couple of rounds of that, I did. Delegated more to the hands, stood and watched them do the cowboying, even though that was always the thing I liked best about the ranch. Stayed off horseback too, most of the time. Took the truck out to the rigs to talk with the drilling foremen, checked the meters at the rigs that were pumping, and drove to Odessa to check on the tank cars. Eileen was away a lot, and when she was on the ranch she was busy with books and accounts and ordering and expediting. God only knew how she had done this alone. Well, not alone. There were the brothers, the ones still home, but they were never much good at anything but the labor, and no help to Eileen.

One day this guy shows up looking for a job, says he's done some cowboying and also some roughneck work. He looked strong, fit, a straight shooter, and I said we'd see and hired him on. Got him started out on one of the rigs we thought was pretty close to coming in. I was out on a visit to that rig on an afternoon that looked like one of our West Texas thunderstorms. I was talking to the foreman about making sure everything was tight in case we caught the storm just as the well came in. We didn't want any blowouts, especially in a storm like that. When I left the shack, the new guy was standing there with his hands on his hips, searching my face.

"You don't remember me, do you."

"No," I admitted, "Should I?"

"Not really, no. Just that we served together in Nam." He looked so sad.

And there it was. "Sack?!" I shouted and hugged him, I was so glad to see him, I didn't care who saw us. He hugged me back, but just a little, then straightened his arms.

He was alive!

• • •

We all called him 'the Sack' after that army guy cartoon strip in the 50s, "Sad Sack". Sacco Bennetti was forever sad looking and even morose. Except when he was singing.

"I'd change her sad rags into glad rags if I could!" He'd cut loose at the top of his voice.

Some of us would chime in with, "Hand me down!"

"Rag doll! Such a rag doll!" he'd scream in an impossible falsetto. It was like being on patrol with Frankie Valle.

"Shut it!" the Sarge would order, and we'd all laugh our asses off until he gave us a look like a broken arm.

When he wasn't doing Four Seasons tunes, he'd be off on the Beach Boys. Little Deuce Coup, and Little Old Lady from Pasadena. Like that. Got all animated. Never more than a couple words, and sometimes we'd do responses with him. And only ever on patrol. And beforehand, and after his outburst, he was the Sack.

He told me and some of the guys once he was a famous doo-wap singer back in the world, had records and everything.

"Yeah," he said, looking extra sad, if that was possible. "Fuckin Army. Drafted me right out of my recording career. Now I'm gonna die in this jungle meat grinder."

"Ain't we all," chipped in one of the guys. And we all nodded our resignation. Sack gave us his sad smile and went off somewhere. I didn't believe him of course. Every second dick was always telling us they were this or they were that, back in the world. It was all part of what I called the 'oh God, I am not here – please, please – I am still in the world' game. I think we all played it at one point or another.

Then one night after a really bad night op – totally FUBAR'd intelligence, Gooks surrounding us, instead of the other way around, lots of shelling, everybody shitting their pants, the Sack losing it really bad. He was balled up on the ground with his hands over his head. I thought he'd been hit so I ran over to him. I'm sure he was not the only one lost it that way. I wanted to do the same thing, but I couldn't leave a guy hit.

He was shaking really bad, and drooling out words that made no sense to me in the midst of all the explosions.

"Sack! Sack! Are you hit? Let me see, man!" I looked for torn fabric, blood, checked his pupils, his pulse, when I could get him to settle down just a bit, "Sack!" I yelled at him. "You're ok! You're not hit! I can't find anything. Take it easy, man. I gotta check the others." And I crawled off looking for others.

Air support showed up really quick for a change, and nuked the mortars and the shelling stopped. Nobody got killed and the only wounds were caused by running blind in terror, though that's not what went into my report. And we all got dusted off back to base.

Later that night he was in the mess tent by himself, or thought he was, a can of brew in his hands, his head kinda down. About as sad as I'd ever seen him. Then he started singing, not falsetto but regular, staying sad, which was not like him, "When I settle down, I want one baby on my mind … ."

Some of the others heard him and came over to stand around outside the tent. "Forgive and forget, And I'll make up for all lost time … ." Then he stood up, and sang into the can, in his high voice, "I can't stop, I can't stop! Because lightning's striking again! Lightning's striking again!" And he throws his head back and slams the can on the table, suds shooting up six feet in the air.

And there's this look on his face. Have to say, it was pure exaltation. Like none of us had ever seen. And he sees us. We'd started crowding into the tent on his chorus.

And one guy says, "You're him! That famous guy, whatsisname!" And there's a chorus of "Yeah!"

"Barry Sadler." says another guy.

"No, asshole, the rock guy!" says another.

"Barry Gibb?"

"No, not goddam Barry anything!"

"Eddie Kendricks?"

"Who?" say several guys all at the same time.

"Christ Almighty!"

"Christ? Christie! Lou Christie – that's it! You him?" I say.

And the Sack just smiles his little sad smile and shakes his head sadly and walks between us and out of the tent.

• • •

"You're alive!" I clap his shoulders.

"Yeah. Looks like you are too. We all thought you didn't make it, Doc." He just looks at me.

I turn to look at the derrick, the sky with its approaching storm. "I almost didn't," I say, too

183

softly, then louder, "Those Navy surgeons know some pretty good tricks!" I clap my own chest for emphasis.

The smile again. "Glad you made it Doc."

"Not a doc anymore, Sack, gave it up." I can't think of anything else to say. Then, "What about you? You were sure you were gonna die in the jungle."

"Me? I guess. Didn't happen. Here I am." He gives a little bow.

"Doing any singing?"

"Not really. Kind of been getting my head together. Figure where to go next. That kind of thing," he says.

We both look up at the rumble from the sky. Look over to where the drilling is going at a furious pace.

"Lightning's striking again ..." he keens in his incredible high voice, his face a bright patch against the looming gray background.

21

Iraq. Al Anbar Province
_/_/2007. The Present.

I don't know why, but I am so tired I can hardly see straight. Couldn't just be the sleep I missed, out in the desert. Not just the long day today. And I can't just go to my tent. I feel like I just don't want to dream. Sitting here though, with the wind down, the night is playing tricks on my eyes. There are voices, music? I scrub my face with my hands. That dampness again, not desert. My gear is soggy. And it's the guy again. Me – but also the old guy, back there. Back then. Vietnam.

And it's like sitting around a campfire in the evening, somebody playing a guitar. This one guy playing raunchy songs with a particular delight. Gandalf, I think we call him. I don't think anyone knows why. Stub of a joint Bogart'd on his lower lip, fingers playing all by themselves.

No fire here though. The only light is the red glow of cigarette ends, and other smokables. It's like he could play blindfolded if he wanted, his granny glasses reflecting the red glints as his head moves to the rhythms of his stories. I know he's told us they first sent him to army language school in California, says he can speak Vietnamese. "I know 33 ways to say 'dead!'"

He drops one song right in its middle, if any of his songs have middles, or ends, to light a fresh joint, and then right back into the middle of something else. None of them make much sense, but I know him, and he is a 'trip,' I hear in my thoughts.

I feel, like before at the stream, that I don't belong here, with these guys. I do not know any of the grunts around me, except this Gandalf, and what I know of him is like I read it somewhere. And I have only the same kind of memory of what we were all doing before this evening. Like I read it in a report.

I can't say anything about this … stuff. I mean when I wake up, or whatever. I might get mental-case'd out of the fighting. But I'm not sure anymore if that would be bad. It is just too weird sitting around in jungle rig, swatting at bugs. I'm trained for desert, not this … this close presence, even this far back of the wire, this closeness of the living, breathing jungle all around us. And everything so wet, it squishes. I almost want to say, 'how did I get here?' but that feels even more nuts.

The music, if I can call it that, stops. The skeletal figure stands, takes off his pot, runs spidery fingers through really long hair (also really stringy), takes the doobie out of his mouth and exhales an impossible long time. He is looking over our heads, out There. Over the wire. "Cinder, I think it's gonna rain," he half sings, to a melody it seems only he knows. "Better get inside and write my letter."

And he goes, taking his ratty guitar with him. We all sit awhile.

"Hijo de puta," says a Chicano guy near me. Brushing off his hands, he stands and walks into the night. "Gonna rain? Fuckin' guy."

I stay. I don't know where to go. Slap a bug on my neck. A big one. And it doesn't squash, it just sorta crunches wetly. The night sounds swell until I almost can't hear my own thoughts. Fucking place. What am I doing here?

And then I'm not.

Rivers is just here, right in front of me, like a ghost. I didn't hear him coming. And he is all by himself, no Blake to be seen anywhere. His dark face is lit only with his trademark leer. "We know it was you took the rug, Bird-man," he accuses, all serious. Then,"Birdman!" he croons softly, almost lovingly. Flaps his elbows. "Fly away Birdman. Fly away with your nasty rug. Fly home to your raghead brothers and sisters!"

I try to get around him, nervously looking for Blake or some of the others, trying not to let him see my fear, trying not to feel it myself, failing at that, at both.

"Oh! They around, Birdman." Him tracking my eyes. "They just don't be flying, like you!" He is going all gangsta-in-the-hood on me, flaps again, staying directly in front of me. "You one strange Marine Birdman. You think you the Lone Ranger or somethin'? Captain America? You think yo shit don't stink?"

I can't move. I feel caught.

He moves randomly back and forth, now in front of me, now along side, maybe almost whispering in my ear, his ghetto accent getting heavier. "I know what you think about us. You think you better than all of us. But you real glad we got yo ass covered when Abdul and Karim is shooting at it. Huh."

I say nothing. I do not think of moving.

"Lemme 'splain somethin to yuh, Birdman." He puts his arm gently around my shoulders and walks me with him, gesturing the whole time with animation, turns off the black guy speak like a faucet. "Guys like you? You think there are great long moments when the pleasure of it doesn't get into your heart, your intestines. You think it's a nasty thing, but somebody's got to do it. Look at you. You know that's not so. You look and see. I mean really look and see, deep down. You know you touch your weapon with a lover's fingers. You know your heart sings when you draw down and squeeze off those first rounds. And the music takes your head, and you give your body to the dance, and you don't know nothin else. You explode with it. Over and over. And when it's done, you only want more. You taste the blood of the dead, and it's your blood."

I cannot speak and I feel like I'm full of snakes. Some deep answering slither in my guts.

"Oh yeah. You know it. I can see it. I can smell it on you." His nose sensual, close to my neck. Then his eyes inches from mine. "It's all over your face." His hand moves so quickly, or I am so deadened, and his fingers caress my cheek, once, and pull away. To return with a slap so hard my teeth crunch together. He gives me a great big smile – it is almost sweet – and then walks away.

My face is a mask of denial and anger. I wear it like something government issued.

And it's the last I ever see of him.

Desperate for sleep, or desperate to disconnect and drop away, I go to my tent and lay on my side and let it take me. There's the usual almost-understandable whispering and the feeling of lying on a sloped earth and slowly sliding over the edge of something, a small dim light show and muted bell tones like distant traffic, and I'm gone.

> *Late night, in a diner on the edge of the desert. The windows completely dark, reflective as mirrors. Catsup, mustard, sugar, salt and pepper in a chrome wire rack off to my left by an over stuffed napkin holder, plate of barely tasted food pushed away. I lift the edge of my right hand again from the table surface and see an oily wetness there where my hand rested while I ate with my other hand.*
> *I take napkins to wipe my hand, but it is dry. I mop the table instead and go back to my meal, pulling the plate in front of me again. In a minute I lift my hand to see the same oily wetness printed with the contours of the muscle and skin of my hand's curled edge.*
> *I lift my hand and long sleeve higher, turning them to inspect them both closely. Dry. No sign of oil or moisture. But there's the same wet*

print on the table. I mop it dry again, extra carefully.

I put my fork down and try to poke the table with a dry finger. No mark. I rest my hand lightly on the table in the same spot. Nothing. I press my hand blade down hard and lift it. There it is. Like it's come from my hand, from a damp sponge. But that hand is dry. And hard.

I think, is the hard fake wood surface of this table soaked, saturated, with an endless supply of hand print juice? I rub the table hard with two clean napkins until there's nothing. Put my hand edge down again, and press. Pick it up, see it is dry as a bone. A wet spot on the table beginning now to fill in, like a footstep in a swamp.

Then something in the middle of me drops with a thunk, and it falls out, through an opening in my chest. Falls and falls, me losing it and going with it at the same time. Down and down.

It wakes me up. Not all at once, but I can tell I'm not asleep anymore, and my fuzzy sight swims into a pattern I can almost recognize.

I'm soaked in sweat, and sit up slowly, letting my surroundings become familiar to me again. Sand everywhere, of course, even in my tent.

There is some serious commotion outside. Not gunfire, not even the shouting of men awakened like a hive of angry bees. Did I miss something?

Two serious-looking guys I do not know are making a path straight for me, both wearing wide black Shore Patrol armbands. One calls out, "Bird, Charles Artemis?" and they both keep coming, right hands dangling so close to their sidearms my insides want to come out my ass.

"Yeah?" I answer and strap on my pot.

"You're to come with us, right now Private." And reading my thoughts, "No questions."

The battalion XO and a captain I don't know who's wearing JA insignia are both standing at the back of the room I've been dropped off in. I give them a decent battlefield salute, since we're indoors, and the XO returns it automatically. "Take a seat Private Bird."

There's just one hassock in the center of the room, and I put my behind on it, take off my lid. My face a big question mark, I am sure.

"This is Captain Liu, Judge Advocate, Private. If you have any legal questions, you can ask him."

"Why would I have legal questions?" I am more puzzled than scared, but still plenty scared.

"You don't know?" The XO pretends to be surprised. Maybe he's not pretending.

"No Sir." They look at me. "May I ask what's happened? Sir?"

The look at each other. The JA, Captain Liu, nods slightly. "Last night there was an explosion in your company area." They both look at me like I ought be saying, 'Oh. Yeah!'

My face is still a big question. "An explosion?" almost like I don't know the word.

They exchange another look. "Look, son, this will go a lot easier if you don't drag it out. We know about the rug. There are witnesses who say you took it." They look at me expectantly. A while. The XO huffs some air and takes a half step toward me, the JA's hand reaching to restrain him, very delicately. "And we know about the bad blood between you and Blake. And Rivers," he spits at me. And looks at Captain Liu, whose eyes do not leave my face.

Images of Blake, Rivers, their gang, the rug, the desert, the fighting and killing in that village all run around and crash into each other in my head. I don't know what my face looks like. I can soon tell what they think it looks like.

The XO's face changes, softens. He folds his arms and leans against the only table in the room. It gives a little under his weight, and he springs up and away from it, arms slashing wide, covering his surprise with a grimace. "Look. Son. Private Bird. We know what it's like out here. We know about Rivers and Blake. We've even been watching them for a while." He pauses, to assess my response, I guess. Which is nothing as far as I can tell. WTF. "We can't condone what you did, son, but we do understand it. Tell us about it."

My mouth, which is already open, shapes some words, but no sound comes out. I swallow. All those images still churning in me. "They were sons of bitches, Sir. Should never have been embedded with us. Disgrace to the Corps. And they killed a lot of non-combatants. Civilians, Sir. Kids, women!" All come tumbling out like a ripped sack of beans. Like guts from a shrapnel wound. I am breathing really heavy, and I want to put my face in my hands. I notice my hands shaking, and then notice I am shaking everywhere.

"You're telling me they're dead, Sir? Is that it?" I search their faces. "Is that it?"

Liu's eyes look down.

Three

"...as gently as we awake from dreams."

Ralph Waldo Emerson
Nature 1836

Intermezzo Primo

I am ripped awake by the slicing cold of night stars in an icy mist. And falling.

The slipping wind of it pulling at my eyelids, my lips. Haze softened stars above and moon frosted billows below.

Not so far below, now.

Glittering in their fall along with me the shards of my sleep – and the airplane we were on. My rushing end squeezes my heart, a cry escapes me, torn away before it reaches my own ears. Where is she?

Is she tumbling lost like me, and just not visible? Or am I alone in the upward rushing night.

Am I numb with the cold? Or is this the dread my heroes never knew? A trick of the stars or of my ears in the stinging ice - all is silent. The waxing lunar sliver on the horizon paints everything with a pallor, at once glowing and faint. Phosphors of the deep, and the dead.

Now floating in silence the wreckage strewn in all directions, there is time for all things. I see the many cerulean hues layered over the swirling ice as if with artist's wet brush. And now not just a mist, but each crystal, void and directionless

*in its sovereign space, black tinged
with milky blueness.*

*She speaks to me now, but not
as from falling. Rather, as the
coruscating background she sounds
against. "Will you bring me back
then? Or will you let me fall?"*

*I have no voice in the
bone-chilling suspension, but my
heart, caught in my teeth, stutters its
reply. "Yes," it says to the first, and to
the second,"No, never."*

*And the blue, the glittering
airliner fragments, all of it, run
down the firmament, while the icy
mist turns to needles of steel against
my cheek, and the chasm yawns
open and inhales deeply.*

Intermezzo Secondo

Sometimes, when I feel all wrung out, I wonder at where I am, how I got here. And maybe where I am going.

Thread of violence? Yeah. What is left inside you after a couple decades of knocking around in your psyche – inputs from kinds and levels of violence you don't even recognize as violence any more … .

There's a lot written about violence, my violence, everybody's violence. When I am completely empty like this, I see a thread connecting all of my past with all of my future, and connecting me with a lot of others, maybe you too.

You ask me if I am a spectator. A watcher in my own life? Well, maybe not. Not anymore. Maybe my own thread of violence is looking for a resolution. Or an outlet.

I am not a voyeur.

notes from sessions with Charles Artemis Bird
by Elizabeth Grain, Ph.D.

Intermezzo Terzo

I see them flying toward me through the air, lazily spinning, flailing.

To land at my feet, wet and crumpled.

Not recognizable. Two great lumps. Like manikins maybe, human shapes, but with parts awry. Heavy, limp legs dangling backwards now over impossibly arched back, all stacked crazily on remains of a face, neck bent back up towards the heels. One of them. Staring eyes, not seeing.

The other. On its side, part curled away from me around the first. Seemingly stopped in a reflexive act of preserving privacy, seeking comfort. Heavy, both of them, with a startling new kind of gravity.

Not manikins.

No motion. Not even a settling.

I have no speech, I make no move. I don't even think, except to briefly and clinically note my own shock.

It's not just the eyes, and the stillness. An utter quiet that spreads, absorbing all other sound, thought, feeling ...

*There's something else.
Something ... absent. But so present,
so intrusive. Anger? Mine, for sure.
Theirs? Their bodies arrested in
impossible, horrific poses ...*

*They scream their shock, their
betrayal, filling a space far larger
than what their remains take up.
Those are small now. Too small. Far
too small for what they had just
been, moments before.*

22

San Luis Obispo
_/_/2007. The Present.

Coleridge's ancient mariner had his albatross. In the Gospels, Matthew speaks about a fatal millstone.

Clayton Ray?

I do not know which is worse, the man himself or the dead tied around his neck.

Maybe I see something there that gives me hope. Maybe such a millstone can be untied, cast alone into the sea.

Or maybe it is a certainty of conclusion. A long plummet with a short memory.

That was it, wasn't it. I wasn't looking to see whether or not he had done this thing, long ago. I was not investigating anything here. I was proving. Proving he had not murdered those men. Proving a man acquitted of the crime had not done it. Because he would not say so himself.

He wouldn't say he hadn't done it. I thought it was because of his need to be believed. Because to offer a denial was for him a form of degradation, the oldest form of degradation, for a race once enslaved. A race assumed to be guilty. Of something.

So he was never going to say. And I was going to prove it anyway, prove the negative. Chase across the decades, to prove he did not do something he would not deny doing. For him? I thought it was for him. Because Tuyet had asked me? But that was not what she had asked.

If Ray was not innocent, at least of those particular charges, and not just acquitted, if Ray was not a heroic figure. Then what was I?

I needed him to be right. To be innocent. To be larger than I was. Larger, and Better. Tuyet sent me to him, but I had made him a mission of my own. And if he had done the murders, even if there was some way it could be justified, in the smoke and stain of war, if I could not prove that he had not? Then, what?

Then there was no hope. No reason. None at all. No reason for me to be doing any of this. No hope that I would ever … be anything but what I was. What I had always been.

An angry man. A killer. Nobody.

• • •

Yes. I had killed. And somewhere inside, I wanted to kill more. And I was angry.

Not at first. Not like later. First I *got* killed. Yes. They killed me. Same as. Took the life I had, took – I can hardly bear to think it, even now – took Tuyet. Took me from her. And dead to all, I ruthlessly made her dead too.

So, not at first. At first I thought about nothing but the pain, about stopping the pain. About the collection of parts left behind on my bed. Wired, stapled, sewn, stitched together. With cloth, plaster, tinker toy braces of steel. Raised and lowered like a lazy draw bridge. Wiped, polished, rinsed and emptied. Emptied. Empty. Left-overs.

Mostly, I do not even recall my dreams then, though there must have been hundreds. Thousands. Because waking was unendurable, without the next meds, the next passage into dark dead places. Let me stay, I would pray. Let me stay.

But they would not. They wanted me to sit, speak, then to walk. Clanking, stumbling thing. Like Shelley's monster. All spare parts. All dumb, deaf and sightless. All dead.

Except that I wasn't. I could see, though I did not want to. I could speak and had nothing I could bear to say. And I could hear. *Everything.* And I despaired for being unable to avoid it all.

I was nothing, and I wanted to stay that way.

They had other plans. Rehab. PT. Endless rounds of psychiatric sessions. I could walk. I got stronger. I could answer simple questions. And when I could dress myself and perform basic bodily functions without assistance, they sent me out.

And I blinked. Like a creature spawned and raised in a lightless world, I blinked at the light of the sky. Unsheltered. Twitched at the sound of a world that had simply gone on. 'War's over. Let's get on with it.' And I had no words to hold up, no words to ask what had happened. No words to yell, "You motherfucking sons of bitches! What did you do? What have you done!" To me. To my brothers in arms. To all those civilians. And for what.

Now I was angry. Now I really wanted to kill somebody. And for the first time in maybe forever, it felt good. And the more I felt it, the more I yelled, the more I felt good!

And I found out it was 1975.

I had no plan. I raged. I lashed out. I got locked up. I drifted to the company of other raging people. Many of them in absolute silence. Sometimes I would sort of level out, find a place, maybe even act normal for a while. Do a little work. But it took less and less to set me off. Hit a boss. Break a window. Start a fire.

And they put me away. They. And the meds started. And other things.

After a while, sometimes a long while that I had no sense of measuring, I was given jars of meds, and scrip, and clean clothes and I was sent out. And when my head would clear from the drugged haze, I would start to remember what I was about. My mission. To get them. The bastards. The ones responsible for ... everything. The ones who paid no price, gave no mercy. Took everything for their own. I would remember that I had to get ... at least one of them. And I wanted to. Badly. But who? And my head would expand, and the staples would strain, and the fiery liquid would rush down my arms and up through my aching guts. And I would collapse into my meds, my meds, my meds. Thoughtless, and nearly senseless. And without direction, wander and follow the silent angry.

Until they put me away some more.

And then I would think about getting out. Long for it. Ask about it. Even though I had probably talked like that every time I came back.

And when I'd get released, it still didn't really happen. Looking for them, I mean. I got out, alright. And immediately got lost. Not like clueless on a map. I'd find a place to stay right away, find a place or two to eat, buy some clothes. I didn't really want to be back on the street. I'd say to myself, like a chant, "I will not forget. I will not be back."

Sometimes, when I was on the outside, it felt different. The same stuff would come up for me, every time, and it would make me just want to pull in my head. Only I would figure I couldn't. At least for a while. It was really hard, maybe the meds doing their thing, but it was so hard to keep a picture in my head. That kind of picture. The kind I needed to get the bastards. There were so many other pictures screaming for attention. And forget about it if I did go off the meds.

I could not find my way. I'd stay in a room for days, and when I did go out I walked a long way and talked to no one. I'd start to lose track of time, again. Mostly I guess, I stayed on the discharge meds, and I don't know whether that hurt or helped. I was afraid to throw them away.

I just couldn't get good pictures of the evil bastards to stay in my head, couldn't get a good fire started. Like trying to find VC on patrol. Primed and ready to rock, we were, but no fight. The harder we'd look, the thinner they got. Like ghosts. Like ghosts. Just like the bastards I couldn't find now either.

I'd do odd jobs, not because I needed the money, but just for something to do. And I think I must have met some nice people. Here. There. But nothing seemed to matter. Days just came and went. Weeks. And I wouldn't talk.

I guess I'd just start getting crazy again. And that's why I'd get sent back.

The last time they let me out, I found out it was 2003.

Now sometimes I wonder, just like the beginning of a real plan, where They live, where I can find Them. Or even just one of them. But who would that be? And sometimes I think about logistics. Like how do I get in, take him out, and then get out myself. But it's all just vague, not guided. I guess I don't have the focus to do any of this.

Most of the time? I hate to say it, but it just doesn't look that bad out here. Mostly quiet. Mostly folks doing a quiet thing. It's the newspaper headlines though, and sometimes the occasional TV I run across. If I catch one of them right, the right side of my face goes numb, my guts get a stab of freezing cold, my eyesight gets blurry behind a headache that feels like something is trying to get out. And I cannot get my breath. If I don't shake that off quick, I can spend the next couple days pretty well catatonic, no movement at all, and my mind gone – I mostly don't remember where. And after that, I just want to curl up in a ball.

I don't though. No. I don't.

23

The sun was high and cruel. I was startled to find that my shirt was off, and I was as dripping wet as if I'd just stepped out of a shower. I was dying of thirst but I had no water. Everyone was very busy. I was standing on a small rise in a clearing, and I was not thinking about being shot. Others had their shirts off too but they didn't seem to mind. There was yelling and turmoil, but no one spoke. It seemed there was a lot to get done and not much time to do it.

It went on. I got hotter. My head got fevered. My thoughts blurred, muddied. I was anxious, angry. And now, at last, scared. The pace of everything picked up, there was no breeze, and nothing got done. Then it started over.

Death was minutes away. Our weapons were also minutes away. I could not decide to save myself, or work harder. I worked like a maniac.

*The sweat ran down and soaked my
pants.*
         *In a minute, it wouldn't
matter.*

San Luis Obispo
_/_/2007. The Present.

I had said my own goodnight to Ray and left
that cell. I do not remember going back to my room.
I must have though. I woke up laying on top of the
covers, still dressed. I thought a lot about Ray. Ray
and me. I thought about what I was doing, and why.
I thought about where I had been, for a long time
where I had been. It hurt. In my head, my body. Not
as much as sometimes though. I wondered how long
I had been here, this time, in this room. The drapes
were pulled so I didn't even know what time of day it
was. I had to get out. Outside. Away.

I did go back, near the end of her evening
shift. I went to that place, the restaurant, the one she
works at, to get something ... coffee I guess. And she
was, again ... attentive. And helpful too. She's the one
told me about the big rock, got me started on that
piece of geology, the way the earth moves here. I had
thought of asking her out, part of me wanted to. But
also not. Something else to think about, someone else
to be with? It seemed too much.
But here we are, standing next to this great
thing. Morro Rock.
"Rena," she says.

Stupid. I had not asked her name. She had not mentioned it, until now. I am so tangled up, I don't know if I even want to be here. But it is a warm night.

She offered me my choice of pie, I just shook my head. When she brought my check, she asked me if I wanted to go for a walk. Just like that. What could I say. We drove. I stopped here and we took off our shoes and walked on the beach.

"Rena." I say it like the answer to one of the great mysteries, then hate my voice, think how can I get out of this. This … whatever is happening. I don't want it. Any of it.

She faces me obliquely, takes my eyes, gently. Shakes her head and gives me the smallest smile. No irony. Just … what? I find her hand in mine. And we walk like that, away from the Rock, down the beach a ways.

She asks me nothing.

My hand rests lightly on the front of her hip. The rise of bone just below her waist and to the side. The soft earth of her abdomen's flesh just over the rise. And the waters recede, withdraw around me, as though a great drain has been opened. The tide draws back, far back, impossibly far back. My breath goes out with it. And then begins, slowly at first, rushing back in. And with a mounting rise of heat, a descending rise, from the skin of my breast down, and deeper in, down to the back of my spine and then rushing forward … her mouth open with her own in-rushing tide of air, of heat, of surprise, of recognition. I surf above her, waters foaming, driving, until we are both upended, tossed, rolling, head-over and over. Gasping at last on warm dry sand, our fingers locked together. The sound of the crashing surf only just behind us growing more distant as we lie tumbled, tangled together, alive.

Alive.

24

Her voice calls softly out to me, gently, insistently. I hear the murmur of Pacific surf. She calls again, touches my shoulder. I startle awake, sit up. My head spins. I look down and around me. No beach.

No Rena.

"Charlie."

I look up, toward her voice, her face and body silhouetted against a rising sun. Against a distant shore.

"Charlie."

I know that voice.

"Charlie. It is time for you to come home. You, and Clayton. Home. We are here. We are all here. Come now."

Here? What is this? Crazily my mind computes that the rising sun and shoreline are in the same place, so this must be ... the other side of the Pacific? No. No. I reject that.

And who is this? This form, this voice.

Tuyet.

But here, now? She moves closer, she is wearing her Ao dai. Tuyet? Which Tuyet? No. This can't be.

"Yes, Charlie, it can. It is."

Her hat shades her face, the sun's glare a corona behind her. She is old, and young at the same time. She is Tuyet. And she is Tuyet. She is her daughter's daughter. Granddaughter, and ... No. I can't do this. I won't. I look at myself to see if I am wearing some kind of uniform, different clothing. Carrying a weapon. This has to be another one of those ... those ... visits.

Nothing.

I am wearing nothing. And ... the scent of her on the air, the touch of this breeze ... it is too real to be a dream. Spiders crawl up my arms, the plates of my skull start to crush inwards. "You can't do this to me!" I brush froth from my lips. "I left! I left!" Torrents of tears stream into my mouth so I have to cough them out. "You can't make me come back! I won't! I won't. I ... can't."

I have tipped forward on my knees, my hands and arms reaching senselessly toward her. Fending her off. Or grasping in a hated desperation. I am so ashamed. Of myself, of my anger. Take me away.

I see the sand coming up to meet my face.
"Charlie ... "

... I am walking on a road between villages. It seems I have been walking a long time, the huts of the next village just now coming into sight. I can hear voices and animals.

I cannot remember what I was doing before. Maybe something about an island, a prison. Yes, a prison camp, or what used to be one. On a big island. I had been walking there, in that camp. All vague, murky, like in a dream. Like in some dreams. People used to be there. Captives. Guards. Interrogators. But it had been like a set from a Tim Burton movie. Or a theme park designed by the Marques de Sade. No one there now. Just me, walking. Walking through it. Doors and windows hanging open, empty. Tattered flags and banners fluttering in a breeze off the South China Sea. One flag sticks in my memory. At half mast, brown on top and blue on the bottom. A yellow star in its center. Not tattered. Not fluttering ... .

Now, at the edge of this village I find a small boy and an old man, standing. Waiting. He is so old it seems a wonder he can stand and breathe. And the boy... this boy. I think I know him, but cannot guess how. The old man makes a kind of bow that seems more like a controlled crumple of his whole body. And the boy continues to smile, his eyes fixed on mine.

"Welcome stranger. You come far," he says in English. Or at least that's how I understand it. "You seek our village." It is not a question.

I stand, stupidly. I cannot take my eyes from the boy. The old man's words trickle to some place in me that knows them. "Yes." I answer, but no one moves. It is as if movement, or any other action, would be a waste. "Yes," I say again, so I can believe it, "Yes, this village." I hear myself say, but I do not know what I mean. I do not know this village, have never thought about it. I am sure I was never here.

The boy's eyes grow light, then dwindle to tiny points of fire, and he steps behind the old man, only his small fingers visible, gripped on the seams of the old man's shorts.

The old man's eyes become clear, then hollow, as he asks, "Have you ever visited the big island Can Son?" At the end of this question that thuds against my ribs from the inside he is standing much closer to me than before. I did not see him move. "There was a prison camp there. For VC and other dissidents. It was French, later RVN. You called it 'Devil's Island East.'" He smiles. "You should do that while you are here 'in country'." He says that term with a perfect grunt's accent and my stomach turns to hear it, spoken that way, just as we had said it so normally during the war. 'In Country' we'd say, just as if we owned it, or had a lease on it. What arrogance.

"Yes," I say. "I have." But I do not believe what I hear myself saying. There was ... before. Like a dream. But I was not there. Could not have been.

I see surprise in his eyes, now filled in again, just a little, and maybe also a twinkle. "As you probably know, it is now visited annually by former captured VC and their families." He is all silence then for a while, moving, changing clouds gather behind his head as he grows, or appears to grow taller.

Parallel lines begin to stretch out, yearning to meet. Dense jungle foliage superimposed on the clouds, now on the old man, who now grows impossibly younger as I watch. And as I watch, he fades to nothing.

"I was never captured. But I knew many who were." His words come out of a silent rush of such images, so fast I cannot separate them. But I know what they mean. Now he stands with me again, waits for me, but I do not know what to say. "I go each year to pay my respects," he tells me, with a question in the lines of his face. "If that was your mission, than you may find yourself blessed. Otherwise, it will be very dangerous for you now." He smiles. It is a puzzle.

Then, we are surrounded by villagers and swept along. Men and women, young and old. And children. Eyes all full of hungry curiosity. And patience. The old man says nothing and I cannot see where the boy has gone. It is clear I am invited to share rice with them all. It is a strange meal, a new meal for me. It is dense and salty and pungent with the smell of long-dead fish, their protein staple, a sauce they call *nuoc mam*. It tastes good to me. But I slow my eating to match the others I can see, as I look around, silently. I am the only one who is not talking. The small room is filled with animated conversation, none of which I can understand, except for the laughter. They don't seem inhibited by me.

"Do you ever think about how you and I were once enemies?" the old man asks, again in English, and I find he is now just across from me, searching me with his clear eyes.

I think about it, and tell him "Yes." Then, "I mean no. I mean I never thought about you in particular. To me, you were all … the same." I am embarrassed to say it.

"Ah. Yes," he says with a small nod. "But we were," he insists. "Enemies. Once, a long time ago, we were. I fought for my country, my land. You fought for yours."

There are thoughts that want voice. I had not fought 'for my country' in the same way that those words might be said of him. I don't know what I fought for, but the safety of my country was never at issue. My thoughts cascading in long chains of memory, into the machinery of which I've just jammed a wrench, I decide to keep to myself. And I hide their dark ghosts as best I can.

He studies me. I suspect he can read at least some of what I am holding back.

He pulls his near empty bowl toward himself and leans out over it, his face closer to me. "I was a demolition expert. A sapper, you called me." He nods in self agreement.

His eyes hold mine, waiting. For my signal to continue? I cannot tell.

"There was a mission. An incursion, you would say. To strike fear and sow "disaffection," we were told. These strikes troubled me even then, all of them, designed to catch the enemy without warning." Though his gaze on my face does not vary, there is something interior in it for a moment. "They have always troubled me. But I was a good soldier. And I agreed with driving out the invaders – you – by any means." That waiting-to-proceed look again.

I say nothing, but try to look steadily back at him. I am no match for him.

"There were many deaths. Many men killed by me. Brave men, I have no doubt. And all suddenly destroyed. *Chet roi.* Troubling. On one mission, I came up from our tunnels and I picked out a barracks, not unlike my home here in the Highlands, in what your generals seemed to regard as unassailable fortifications. I came up on it one night to blow it up. I wanted to use a US grenade, to add to the confusion, but there were none available at the time, so I had a Chinese grenade with me, one the Soviets had made.

The old man's tale seems to run down. It's as if he flows out of himself and into his bowl, and he sits hunched a little, staring into it. And I let him be. I have my own bowl to look into.

Then with seeming renewed intent and something else I cannot identify but which carries a threat that I feel in my gut, he says, "I came up inside the base perimeter as I often did, and around several groups of tents and hooches, and stood in some cover watching my target to be sure of it. Then I did my work and quickly left." He slides his empty bowl away and leans in again.

"And then there was a thing so strange to me, among so many things that were strange then. As I made my escape, and just before the grenade detonated, I turned to look back, a thing I never did, before or since, and I saw standing right at the door to the hooch a *nguoi toi* – a black man. With his arm outstretched, and suspended. I did not wait to see what happened next. The expected blast came very quickly, and I made my way back to my team, and never knew whether the man was taken in the blast with the unlucky occupants of the hut."

A picture of Clayton Ray springs to my thought, forbidden even as I see it form. It cannot be. He wasn't there. I frown but say nothing.

The old man nods his head as if he has received some kind of confirmation. "You know this man." It is not a question. "Does he live?"

I do not know what to think, or say. I sit silently, my rice forgotten, apprehensive of the now deadly mien of this old soldier, about whose long ago duty he speaks with such a present sense.

Then he begins to grow thinner, lighter. And then transparent, revealing the boy standing behind him, until I can see the boy's eyes, smiling. Just those eyes, points of fire.

And nothing else.

25

I am walking alone. The road is dirt, dry. There are few trees in sight, mostly scrub grass, patches where it looks like dirt has filled in holes.

I thought, I really did think, that just once … . And never again. Just once, would be alright. No one would miss him, no one would know. And it had to be done, before he could do anything more horrible.

And when it was done … when it was done, it did not matter that no one knew. That no one would ever know.

I knew.

No, it wasn't guilt – nothing so easy. I never felt anything about that.

But I knew something now about myself. That would never change. I knew that there would be one more. And then another. That it would never get better.

But it would never get any worse.

James A. Haley Veterans Hospital
Tampa, Florida
_/_/2007. The Present.

When I started looking for guys to tell me that Ray really hadn't done the fragging, and I was looking for Vets that had served with him, or with me, I found out from different stories some of the guys had told me that my platoon had been responsible for "pacifying" a particular village just a few days after I got hit and medivac'd out. I am sure I did not get all the details, didn't want them either. But I gathered that by rare good fortune a genuine VC village had been discovered and destroyed. And a VC unit flag captured and retained by my old buddies. Of course it would have been much more likely, either due to the usual faulty intel or operational screw-up, or to the fear and anger of a combat op gone bad – more likely that the unlucky village had just been creamed for no good reason at all. Except maybe for finding that flag there.

I had put all that kind of stuff into the giant mental footlocker I still maintained from those days for shit I never wanted to think about again. But I hadn't ever heard about that village, or the flag, until I learned that it had been passed from man to man in that platoon until all of them had either been killed or rotated out (or sent home in pieces like me), and the last of the guys, a tough old staff sergeant named Alberto Canalari, took it home with him.

It's like I could keep that whole business separate – questions about this vil or that – ours, other units I had heard of – even more separate than all the rest I left behind. But that flag? On US soil? I couldn't let it go. I had to go see it. Touch it. I didn't want to, I had to. And it came to me that I'd have to go find it. The flag. I couldn't get it out of my head.

The Sarge was hard to find. Until I started combing the VA hospitals.

"I always thought you should have it, Doc. I mean, we took it the day after they sent you home. Couldn't have done it without you." I turn away my face to look someplace other than his bed, embarrassed at what looked like real love in his moistened eyes. No, it must be the effect of his medications, I tell myself.

"Ah, you keep it Sarge, you did all the work." I tell him, not adding 'and all the killing.' He didn't need to hear that. Not from me anyway. Definitely not from me. And not anymore.

I unroll what he had had the nurse hand to me and look at it. Rough spun cotton mostly, or maybe hemp, with silken inlays and chasing on part of the borders, where they weren't shredded or burnt. It is grimy, but I can feel something else in it. Some kind of power. Or memories, lodged within the weave? The touch of it asks me to look at the strength of purpose of those who had carried it.

In the middle of two horizontal bands of color is a faded yellow star, arms outstretched, reaching for the edges. A milk-chocolatey brown on the top and the most sublime sky blue on the bottom. A color that took me back to a day at base camp when it felt like the war had come to a stop. No Hueys coming and going, no shooting. Not even the sound of a work detail. I was laid back on my poncho looking up at that sky, wondering, I think, what I would do with the rest of my life. If I had one. That kind of blue. I am thinking it is maybe the most beautiful color I have ever seen.

"We wrote on the back there – see? We wrote the village we found it, and map coordinates." He is pointing, feebly, then lays back, exhausted by the effort. I put a hand on his arm to steady him. He turns his head away to wipe his eyes on the sheet.

I look at the writing on the back, and the ghost of an idea comes into my head. I can take it back. It scares me enough to get brusk with my old platoon mate. "I see that. Kontum, right? Near An Khe?"

"Nuh. I don't remember now. It says there, don't it?"

They hadn't 'found' it. Unless you count sorting through the burned wreckage of hundreds of years of lives as finding. God only knows what infraction they had committed to bring down fire and death. I guess the flag sort of proved something. After the fact. It was a VC unit flag, maybe decades old when it was taken, maybe going back to before the wars with the French and the Japanese. That village could have been home, or at least home base, to people who had been fighting for as long as any of them could remember. And proud to be doing it. Whether they were VC or not. And that flag, mostly never displayed in the open, mostly hidden, had been a symbol of that pride.

"Yeah, it does, Sarge." His eyes are anxious. "Ok," I pretend to relent, "I'll take it. Keep it safe. Thank you, old buddy."

A long sigh escapes him, and all the pain seems to go out of him as his eyes close. Old training makes me leap to check his pulse, he's gone that still.

But he isn't gone. Not yet. The nurse gives me a sour look.

"Take good care of it, Doc. You deserve it," he breathes softly and almost beneath my hearing, and he is asleep.

Yes, I would take care of it. But what part of it I deserved, what part in it I might have had, might yet have, had my spine twisting as I left his room and closed the door behind me.

• • •

In one of his books, James Lee Burke talks about images of Vietnam that are now history, "ignored by those who only wish to recreate them". I had been having a first hand look at that. Iraq. But we all did, right? Vets anyway. Iraq. Afghanistan. It goes on. 'Our Masters' Voices?' ... boys and now women too, dying on numbered hills in distant places.

And like Burke also suggests, Vets are "condemned to being their own history books - with stories we cannot pass on to others ... ."

26

Crazy.

That's what she sang.

When she thought no one was listening. Patsy Cline. Dear Patsy. Mom loved that song. Except she would mostly cry while she was singin' it. I asked her why once? She looked at me, smiled her little smile, til she'd lost it, then turned away and said it reminded her of me.

There was a way to her singin' it that made me know she wasn't thinkin' of me. The words are all about somebody loving and leaving. First I thought it was maybe Dad she was singin' about. He loved her, I guess. And he left – well he died on her, anyway. But that was about the time I was born, and I don't think she was singin' it back then. I remember a lot from my early years, not always in the right order, and most of it not connected enough to anything else so's I could tell about it.

But I think she started singin' it cuz of Steve. Now Steve's gone. God knows where. But I remember both of them, Mom and Steve, bein' pretty close. Maybe even that close. Until they weren't. Or anyway, until he wasn't. And that's when I first remember hearin' her sing that song, I think. Steve driftin' off long before he left.

Crazy.

So, she's gone too. And that song is still on my mind. I hear her singin'. Not a great voice, not like Patsy, but full of feelin'. And sometimes lately, when my desk is full of books and accounts, or I got a truck out alone by one of the pump rigs, and I think about Artemis ... up and quit the place and rode off into the North – and me still too young then to do anything about it ... . I think like that, and I find I got that tune, and some of those same words, comin' outa me. Along with the tears.

Crazy.

Iraq. Al Asad Airbase
_/_/2007. The Present.

These ... things that are happening to me. Dreams. Visions. Sometimes, like now, I only hear them, in my head. It's all just crazy. Like this one, a woman's voice, in my head. And I can even hear the tune of that song. A song I don't know, even though it haunts me. Who is she? And who are 'Dad' and

'Steve'? And 'Artemis'? (That's my name, isn't it?).
Why do I get the idea it's *his* sister, the old guy's.

But it's not more crazy than the other stuff
that I see and hear all the time in this war.

And, for the other stuff, the old guy? I have
been right there in the jungle with him, in his boots.
And other places. More than once now. I feel like I
have to pay attention.

• • •

I am walking with a bunch of people in white
lab coats. I see I am wearing one too. We are
following some guy with a clipboard down a hallway
with a polished floor and lots of doors with wire
mesh in their little windows. We are outside one
now, but I cannot see inside. Only clipboard guy can,
really. He is talking at us.

"See? There he is. He's quiet now. We watch
him pretty closely, monitor his meds." He looks at all
of us. To see if we're taking notes? I don't know. "We
don't have outbreaks anymore." He checks
something on his clipboard and nods to himself.
"Now he presents an interesting variation on the not
atypical solipsistic isolation that goes with a lot of
our disabled war vets. He says he remembers his
fighting in Vietnam, which is of course natural, and
mostly helpful in his therapy. But he also raves about
Permian landmass shifts and the formation of Eden."
Everybody stares blankly at him. I guess that is the
usual response. "You know? The Garden? Oh, and he
says, and we think he believes, that he 'transports' to
Iraq to become a US Marine, 19 years old. Iraq, for
Christ's sake. Unbelievable. Saddam Hussein, Iraq?
What would Marines even be doing in the middle of
that."

A Marine. In Iraq. Is he talking about me? Is this guy in there talking about me? I stay behind as the guy with the clipboard turns away and moves on down the hallway, the buzz of his lab coat group following along behind him.

And now I am inside the room with this old guy. Well, maybe not old, but he sure looks pretty well used up. He looks at me but he doesn't seem much surprised to see me in front of him. It smells bad in here, not just hospital smells, but other stuff? Old clothes? Not unwashed, but soaked with something that maybe doesn't wash out. Something nagging that comes out of the skin? There's nothing in here with him but a cot. He moves a loose arm to show me a place to sit on it, I think. So this is the guy? The same guy from the jungle, but after? After a lot of shit. Well, not after maybe, 'cause it looks like he's still deep in it.

I notice he is speaking. Not to me exactly, and I cannot tell if he just started or has been going on for a while and I did not notice. He is looking mostly at the fingers of his right hand.

"Before I came here, I was on the streets for a long time. I don't remember now how long. They don't like to talk about it, but Jeanie? My group leader? She tries to encourage me." He looks up at me, just a glance, like to check if I am following, then back to his hand and then to the floor. "I like her. I don't care so much about the others in my group. I think some of them are vegetables. And some others are seriously messed up. The rest are just boring." He keeps looking at the floor, here and there, like something may have rolled away on it and is lost in the glare of its polished shine.

"They say, when they think it is safe to tell me things like that, they say that I was violent. On the streets. Shouting out loud to people in the middle of the day, stopping them, asking them questions. Fighting cops when they arrested me. Throwing things. Starting fires. I don't remember any of that, at least no details. I do remember being angry. All the time." He turns his head to me with a very thin smile. "Besides, it's always safe to tell me things." The almost smile fades and as he turns to look away from me, he says quietly, "I am only dangerous when I am alone."

He sits like that a long time, facing away, looking at the wall, looking far away, as if that wall isn't there. Then when I am wondering first if I should leave, and then if I could leave, he stands up and walks past me around the end of the bed and stops under a high window that also has wire mesh in it. The only window. There is nothing to see but sky. From the inside of this cage. Only now it is me looking through the chicken wire at the sky too, and it is my voice that is talking, I can tell. The shift is making me dizzy. I am him again, so it is my mouth moving, my lungs pushing out the words, but they are not my words, and I cannot help it.

I hear as if I were standing right next to him. No, as if I were inside him.

"They brought me here to protect me, but also to protect themselves. I spend a lot of time now zoned out on the meds, but not as much as they want to think. I also spend a lot of time away from here, which is good for them, but they don't believe that. They tell me here that it's just normal for someone like me, someone with PTSD – and a lot of medications – to have dreams, memories, visions ... and that I do not have to worry now about sorting them out. They have no idea.

"And that's good for them, for everybody I guess, because I haven't stopped being angry. Or afraid. Afraid to be alone. Afraid I will make up my mind to kill someone. Afraid maybe I already have. I mean, again. Here. In the world. I haven't said that out loud yet, though I have said it to myself dozens of times.

"When I am not asleep, or traveling, it seems like, sometimes, everywhere I look, my eyes jitter and stick like an ice pick does when it is scraped across linoleum. And then every thought in my head drives me to picture the faceless bastards again, safe in their offices, their homes, the ones who started it. The ones who start everything, getting away with it, thievery, destruction, murder, all of it. And to picture the wreckage they leave behind, the dead and the destitute, the enslaved and brainwashed masses. To see all the misery with an unnatural and mind-ripping clarity. Like stoking the fires of a hell I cannot wait to send them all to."

The room is silent. Not a sound. I am still looking up and out. I want to turn and look to see if I am still there, on the bed, but I cannot.

27

Fort Ord, California
1972

(From the transcript of the court martial of
Clayton Ray ...)

*Are you trying to tell us you
do not know where you were all that
night, Private Ray? That you were
'wasted', in your tent, but just do not
recall? Do you expect us to believe
that?*

*I don't expect your white ass
to believe anything I say.*

*Private Ray, if I have to listen
to anymore of that kind of language,
I will hold you in contempt of this
tribunal and have you put in solitary
for the duration of the trial. Is that
clear?*

Yes. Sir.

*Good. Major, you may
proceed.*

*What <u>do</u> you recall about that
night, Private Ray?*

(Pvt Ray says nothing)

Hmm? I'm sure we are all eager to hear about it?

We were on call all day, supposed to go out in the hump and relieve the 4th Battalion. Waiting. All day. It's worse than going in low on a Huey with incoming rifle fire. Worse than wading neck deep in leeches to get to some real estate no one really wants. Waiting, and waiting. And you know it don't end at night, right? Like waiting while you sleep – is just no sleep at all. And empty bunks, that aren't empty, waiting for you to join 'em.

Well I said, "Fuck that!" Sorry, your Honor. I said, "hell with that" and I lit up.

Nothing changes you know? You guys are all straight, right? Well, I don't know what you heard, but nothing goes away. Nothing. But you stop caring, somehow, or maybe it's just you stop running, running in your head. And you stop. And listen. And the scary shit – I mean the bad stuff – it's still there, but it's, it's like, not sneaking up on you anymore. All together. Just there. Deadly, sure. But not scary.

So, I'm passing around a couple J's with the guys, and – some of them get weird shit – I mean bad stuff – mixed in – and the next thing

*I know it's morning. First Sergeant's
yelling his head off to fall in, and we
all bust ass to gear up, check out
ammo, and haul balls to the
company LZ.*
> *That's what you mean by,
"you weren't anywhere near the
officers' tents?"*
> *Yeah – yes. Sir.*
> *And that's it? Anyone can
corroborate your story, verify you
were in the tents all night?*
> *Only the other G's that were
wasted with me.*

Iraq. Al Asad Airbase.
_/ _/2007. The Present.

It's uh … one of those … dream things again. I
guess. No, not really dreaming. I'm awake. More like
seeing, without looking.

Where does this all come from? Why can't I
just have regular memories. My own memories.

I just want to get this all over with … .

> *I'm walking with a pretty girl.*
[My sister? Why do I think that. No …
she's more than that to me, here]
*We're walking in what is left of an
old western town, stopped at the
window of a shop.*
> *There looking back at me from
the window is the framed front page
of an old newspaper. Yellowed, faded*

with age. Against a backdrop of old cactus, low hills and rolling weeds, the face of an old man, centered and just turning away from staring out of the frame. It's like he, the old man, has just stopped moving. Or maybe he's just begun. Caught in a camera flash.

Across the top of the page, there's the banner "Babylon Trumpet" and the date 1901 with a headline that runs, "West Pecos Man Discovers ... ." The rest of the line and the words below that are too hard to read. Too faded with time and dirt I guess. Off the man's left shoulder, the post of some awning, the rise of a step. A raised plank walkway, like in an old western. And the end of a hitching rail.

I turn away from the paper and sense at the edge of my vision ... something ... like shifting sand, like storm winds rising. And the face of the man in the paper is not turning away, but just completing a turn back. Toward me. A face I know. His face.

And with the wind, I hear an offer. To take me back ...

CMC - San Luis Obispo
_/_/2007. The Present.

Ray told me he'd go back, himself, if he could.

All those images of that country, of Tuyet. Of both of them. Sounds from then alive now in the silence of this room. Everything spinning in my head, in front of me. Ray's eyes on me. Staying on me.

Somehow I thought I had to tell Ray. What I was thinking about doing with that flag. That it felt like I had to take it back. I went once more to visit.

"I was there, like you," he says, as if maybe he already knows what I have come to tell him. "You know what that was like. I didn't think of anything then, in the jungle, on the plains. Nothing except killing whitey, getting high, screwing my dick off and staying alive. Staying fucking alive." He watches me. "I missed it all. I missed so much. I had no idea. Did you?"

"No. Of course not," I answer him. "Like you said, in the middle of all that, how was I supposed to see anything, know anything. Every minute of every day, I … what you said. Mostly. Well, not the whitey part. Or getting high." And for me, I did think there was someone special.

"Yeh. Well. That was the trick, wasn't it." He leaves me then briefly to find a place to sit, and when he does, it's as if most of the air goes out of him, and he looks suddenly ten years older. He looks up at me again. "You ever thought of going back?" He looks at me with his eyes, tired, but all attention, taking me in.

"No," I tell him quickly, too quickly. He doesn't blink. "No, not really. Are you kidding? Me go back to where they killed my ass? Why would I do that? In a million years?" Now I can't just tell him what I am thinking, why I have come to him.

He waits. Without gesture, without a breath. If I could believe his eyes, without a judgment.

"Ok, shit. Yes. Hell, I thought of it. Yes I think of it." I am caught up in caution, reticence. "But I wouldn't do it. Not for anything. I just can't stop thinking about it though. It's like there's a pull. Some kind of gravity. Like I'm on a little slope, a hard stone slope, covered with fine sand, and this pull, see? This pull has me sliding along on that sand. A very little bit, an inch maybe, at a time. An inch maybe in a week. I can't shake it off. I can't – make my feet take hold and stop. For good."

His lined brown face has not changed, except maybe to become a little smoother as I go through this last bit, about the sand and stuff, but I'm pretty sure I see the rise of a smile in his liquid eyes.

"Yeh, like gravity. Just like that. You can stay away. You can hang onto a pole. You can even build yourself a little platform on top to stand on. But the pull never stops. You let go, you step off, you fall. And you don't have to go. No. But nothing will ever take away that pull. Almost nothing. There's this," he gestures with his palms turned inwards, his fingers fanning his own breast, his face, making a surprisingly graceful, even elegant, picture of his old self, framed by the backdrop of that sterile room. "There's this. I still have time left to serve, and now the docs here say I might not even make that." He crosses his arms on the table, a gentle relaxation into the inevitable. "That pull will never stop for me. But no power on Earth will ever bring me there now. Not in this life."

I couldn't take all that in. Him agreeing with me about gravity. For me. For him. That he was sick now in a way I just could not have imagined or expected. I knew he'd never say more about it.

Ray wasn't ever going to get there.

28

Iraq. Al Asad Airbase.
_/_/2007. The Present.

"Ok, Marine, you got a visitor. Be nice to her." And with a jangle of keys, he opens my cell door and points down the hall, his eyes on mine. "Do I need to put on the restraints?"

It takes me a second to think what he's talking about. Then I get it. I'm arrested for murder, so I might try to run for it. "No Sergeant, I'll be good." I meet his eyes.

He nods, turns and takes my arm, like I don't know my way out after all. We walk like that, him now as silent as the walls we pass. Me with nothing else to say to him. My visitor? Who is it? How is that even possible? Is it my appointed lawyer?

We turn a corner, walk some more and turn into a room with its door open. Marks is standing by a chair, on the other side of a folding table. She sees me come in, but there is no sign of it on her face, in the length of her body. She is looking extra sharp.

My escort let's go of my arm and tells me as he is turning, "Fifteen minutes." And the door closes.

I don't know what my face is showing, but I am glad to see her. I walk over to the other chair, hesitate, then offer my hand to her. She looks at it.

Like she is trying to recall what linkage attaches it to my arm. She takes it quickly then. It is firm, and very brief, and she sits down. I do too.

"Uh." I have no words.

"You look good," she says and quickly looks away. There is nothing else in the room, not even a window, and she realizes the bad tactics and turns her head back to face me. "The guys said to say thanks."

"Thanks?"

"Sure. For taking out the trash." Those analytical eyes of hers. Not taking me apart, just watching the gears move.

"Huh." I look at the table. Nothing. "Well that's nice, I appreciate the gratitude." I look up at her. "But I don't think I'm the one that did it. I mean, I don't think so. I don't remember."

Her lips straighten to a line, and I thought they'd already been damn straight. And she flicks her nose up and her chin forward an inch. Silently telling me she hears me and she's staying out of it. Then she looks down at her hands. That surprises me.

"I don't remember." I look at my own hands. My left hand. "How can that be?" I look up at her. She's watching me. No response. Of course not. "You'd think I'd remember something like that, even just a part of it? Or I would remember that I didn't do it. You know?" Now I can't tell if she can even see me, like she's off somewhere else. Just her face left behind. Pointed at me. "You know? When there's a string of memories of stuff you did, you know, just did, and the thing you're supposed to have done isn't in there?" Still watching. Still no response.

"I don't know. Maybe I don't care. I think they got exactly what they deserved. Maybe all that bad luck with the rug caught up with them. They had it coming." I feel my heart reaching across, wanting her to agree with me, say something. Anything.

Nothing. But with her, that nothing is a thing.

"Who's to say we don't all have it coming. I mean, I was there. I didn't stop it. And so what if I did eventually take that rug away from those bastards? I haven't had a chance to return it. And maybe even then, so what. I'd still have it coming."

You can't tell anything with Marks. Still not a sign. But if I had to guess, I could almost say she was fighting with something. With herself?

"Yeh, so? Bad luck? Is that what all of this is? Bad luck? Me here, fighting, like I've never done anything else? Like I cannot remember ever doing anything else? Blake? Me getting thrown in with him and the rest of his scum? And the rug. The rug. Huh. Now they think I did it. Took the bastards out. And it's all on me?"

She stands up, turns away.

"Just the bad luck." I say to her back.

She steps easy over to a wall, just like there was a window to look out of, and she's looking out it. "Do you think maybe there are hollow spaces in each of us? Already sprinkled with cement, waiting for the right kind of moisture to seep in and harden us up?"

Marks. That's her alright. I turn in my chair to face her back. I have no idea what she is on about. "Cement?" I try out.

"What?" She turns her head toward me.

"Nothing. What you said. About the cement?"

She looks out the 'window' again. Like. "I don't believe in bad luck. Or good. There's just me. And you." Then she sighs. A great big, shoulder shaking sigh. I almost fall out of my chair. What's this? Emotion? I stand up so quickly, the chair squeals on the floor. I catch it. She's turned on a dime. Stops me in my tracks with her look, her right hand fisted tightly.

I hold onto the chair. What is going on, I think to myself. Like I don't know (I don't really, but God help me, I think I do). She makes up her mind, I can tell by her gaze getting really hard, harder than it was already. And she marches right past me, to the door, and hits it once with that fist.

I'm turning to follow her. As the door opens, she points a finger at me, stopping me again. "Charlie … " is all she gets out. I can see the sergeant behind her. And her eyes. I almost cannot believe it. There is moisture there, in that desert of a gaze that she uses for a face. And in that second it all lets go. Her guts pull at her shoulders. Her eyes pull down at the corners, the rigid line of her lips, gone. Tears. My god. Tears, streaming down her cheeks. Her impossibly beautiful cheeks. The guy puts his hands gently on her shoulders (and he doesn't die?) and starts to turn her, and she shakes free of him and takes a half step toward me and screams "Char--lie!" She bends forward like she has a cramp, fists tucked into her gut. I feel like I'm breaking in half. And before I can even think to move, she's gone.

29

San Luis Obispo
_/_/2007. The Present.

Everywhere I look in the affairs of the world, there is patronage and influence. No different than it was in feudal times. And of course when those are not sufficient for the powerful and the privileged to gain sway, then threats. Then force. Then, the unspeakable.

Today, a thousand years ago. If man had been allowed by the creator to walk upright when the planetary plates had shifted to their present configuration, it would all have been with them there too. Part of the genealogical code for human.

But the loss of Eden was different, if the stories are true. Adam and Eve walked out alone. Defiant, unrepentant. Their crime one of seeking knowledge at the level of God. No one influenced them (though a shadowy Lucifer is usually blamed). No one paid them off, or threatened their family. In the midst of splendor, grace and beauty the like of which, it is said, will never again be seen on Earth, they demanded to know, to question even the Almighty. And were expelled.

So maybe the racial imperative to seek Eden, to return to it, is not a quest for beauty, or even peace. Maybe it is a human imperative to question, to demand answers. And though a return was denied once and for all at the Eastern Gate, our heredity drives us to search for, to find, an Eden where such questions do not spell eternal exile. Some different Eden.

Iraq. Al Asad Airbase
_/_/2007. The Present.

"This Article 32 hearing will come to order."

I am standing to attention at a table. It is happening again. I know where I am, and vaguely why. I do not know how I got here. I do know it is real. This is no dream. It's him, again. The Marine. Except right now it's me. And I know things that only he would know. When I look, when I sort of feel around in my/his head though, I do not know what happened.

He does not know what happened.

Wait. A little bit. A tent? IED? Blake and Rivers dead. And a rug. A special rug. My head is seared with pain like a split in my skull. I stand tall. There is a woman standing at the table with me, an officer. The man who spoke is also an officer. A Marine officer.

"This is an Article 32 hearing, Private Bird. Do you understand your rights?"

"Yes sir," I hear myself say. I turn to look at the officer beside me. She looks straight ahead. I think we must have talked, but I have no memory of it. He has no memory of it.

There are few other people in this very hot room. The woman, I assume, is my appointed lawyer.

There is another officer at another table, and what I guess is a court reporter seated near the man who is speaking. He has a table too.

"Good. Let's begin by reviewing the specification. You are accused of the willful murder of two fellow Marine security embeds, Blake and Rivers. On a night with no apparent enemy action, and your unit, including you, were in camp, there was an explosion in or near the tent in which Blake and Rivers were bivouacked, resulting in their deaths. Your appointed counsel has entered a plea of not guilty. Is that all correct?"

The woman beside me speaks. "The record speaks for itself, sir. The accused cannot be compelled to comment."

"Noted Captain. Will the accused be testifying at this time?"

"The accused reserves the right to testify on his own behalf, but declines to do so at this time."

"Very well, take seats," says the guy up front.

I assume he is some kind of military judge and jury. I never had any court martial experience when I was in Vietnam. I have no idea how this works. And I still have no idea what happened. Or why I am here. Or how.

"Counsel, under special rules regarding battlefield conditions, I have before me the sworn depositions of a number of witnesses. You have copies. Are you entering any objection to testimony by deposition at this time?"

"Not at this time sir. The accused of course reserves his right, should the matter be referred to a court martial, to confront his accusers and each and every one of the witnesses. It will be the accused's position that, taken in the worst light against him, the accumulated testimonies here do not amount to a case for a trial of the accused on the specification."

"Also noted, Captain. Private Bird, Gunnery Sergeant Pugh testifies that he witnessed an altercation between you and one of the deceased, Private Blake, over a certain rug. I believe it was common knowledge that this rug was taken from a rebel village. Gunnery Sergeant Pugh also testifies that he broke up that confrontation on the verge of a fight."

"Sir, with respect, and without admission, you are not suggesting that a Marine about to have a fight is anything but a Marine about to have a fight, are you?"

"Captain, I am not suggesting anything. I am attempting to gather and assess the weight of evidence relative to the specification. May I continue?"

"Yes sir. Thank you sir."

"Gunnery Sergeant Pugh's testimony is corroborated by nearly a dozen other witnesses to the same incident. I propose they be entered at this time, without reading them aloud. Any objection?"

"No sir, I have read them."

"There are a similar number of witnesses who heard the accused say that he thought he ought to take the rug away from the deceased and return it to its rightful owners."

"Sir, may I refer you to the regulations regarding the taking of prizes during combat and those regarding the possession of stolen property? If Private Bird was angry, even upset, about the deceased's possession of, even abuse of, an illegally obtained and maintained prize, there can be no fault in that, can their be, sir? In fact, wouldn't such anger and resolve be the kind of behavior we would expect of a good Marine, sir? I'm sure I could find and enter dozens of statements about the notorious conduct of the deceased, sir."

"Captain the deceased are not now being, nor can they be, charged with any violations of the UCMJ. But even granting your point that the accused might have been justified in his anger, perhaps even doing his duty, at least as he saw it, don't you see that it only adds to his motive for the acts of which he is charged? And I also have here the depositions of the accused's comrades and his commanding officer to substantiate and verify that the rug was indeed taken and is no longer to be found in the company area."

"With respect sir, I must object. Such testimony calls for unwarranted speculation. If we grant that the rug is now gone, we must also agree that it could have been taken by anyone, and that there is no evidence that Private Bird took it."

"That is correct, Captain. But it goes to the weight of the evidence, and a Court Martial may properly consider it, along with the rest of the evidence. Unless you are planning to enter evidence that someone else did take it?"

"Not at this time, sir."

The rug. I do remember taking it. Now. I mean, I have a memory of it, walking into the desert with it. Along with a memory of wishing them both dead with practically every step I took. I am wondering if I am required to say so now. Or if I should say so whether I am required to or not. I know if they ask me, this Marine, he will not lie.

"Moving on. We also have as a fact that the accused is so far unable, or is perhaps unwilling, to account for his movements on the evening of the acts charged."

"Sir, there is no evidence of Private Bird's unwillingness to provide an account of his movements. It is only true that so far, he appears to be unable to recall anything from that evening. In all other respects, sir, Private Bird has been most cooperative with this investigation, and has been noted as a model confinee since his arrest."

"Yes, well, we'll leave that as it stands. No infringement of the rights of the accused is intended, Captain.

"Now, as to means. The investigation of the explosion itself is not yet fully complete, but all the preliminaries point strongly to the explosion being caused by what is known in this war as an IED, a simple, even crude, explosive device, easily manufactured from materials readily available on a battlefield. And it is well known that every combat Marine knows what they are and that each one of them possesses the skills to make and place such an explosive to deadly effect."

"Sir." She is rigid with what I can only suppose is self control. She takes an extra breath. "Really, sir. With all due respect, that is really too much. To go from 'every Marine knows how to kill', to 'Private Bird did it'? Sir, we really must object most strenuously. This is the farthest reaching assertion of circumstantial evidence!" She practically shouts the last of this. There is a heavy silence in the air.

The judge, or whatever he is, seems to be considering. Then, "Your zeal does you credit,

Captain, and your outburst is accepted for what it is. However." He takes his time looking among his papers. "I have here a deposition from the Provost, just received, here is your copy, reporting that amongst the accused's possessions at the time of his arrest, was a small contact switch taken from a digital wrist watch. Together with a report from Ordinance that such a switch would be effective for use in such an IED."

The lawyer turns to look at me. I mean him, the Marine. At us.

What have we done.

30

San Luis Obispo
_/_/2007. The Present.

In Babylon. Yes. But there are two of them, aren't there.

So, which one. The town near where I grew up? In Estacado County, Texas? Or the legendary domain of towers in the land of Eden?

I was born in the first, and the way things are going, it looks like I (we – the boy and I) may die in the second.

It's Babylon, Texas that is listed on my birth certificate, or so I am told. It is a small town in the Estacado ranch and oil country below New Mexico. It was an ancient escape for me, a place apart from the hateful ranch on which I was raised. The picture show, the diner and drive-in near the center of town, girls, hot-rods, all had gravity for me, to pull me from my orbit as 10th and most distant planetoid from the paternal god and sun of our empire's solar system. That I loved that town says less about it than it does about how much I hated my home.

And of course (I have heard it said, 'Alas') there is no more Babylon. Queen city of the Desert. I am told there are ruins to explore, mostly already picked-over through the centuries by the minions of the wealthy in their archeological 'digs'. Plunderers.

These ruins, and the stories wrapped around them, all stand on or near the banks of the Euphrates River, south of present day Baghdad, and not so far north and west of what I gather is at least one of the favored locations for the ancient Garden of Eden.

In my dreams, or whatever these excursions, these transits are, I run the deserts of Iraq, in company with brave men and women, tough and true. And though we do not extend our travels to this historic site, it lays large in my thoughts. I'm still having that nagging sense of being a tired old man, trapped in a young man's body. Maybe trapped is not the right word. Maybe more like surprised. Or excited? A little. I feel, again, like I know more about the danger we've been facing than I have a right to - even with my long ago combat experience. Know more about it, and well, thrilled too. Scared, yeah. But excited, even eager, to fight again, let it all rip. And I don't think he feels the same way now.

I feel like it is me imprisoned here, and somehow I do not expect to leave this place in the company of my life.

So, what is it that brings me, and as far as I can tell, me alone to these twin reflections. Two Babylons. Is it the deep oil reserves? The tectonic link they shared? That they have in common?

• • •

I sit up, or try to, tears running down my face, my own voice ripping the darkness, "Nuhhh, nuh nuh, nuh! Nooooo! Oh no." My legs are tangled in sheets, one arm held down ... Rena?

She stirs, rolls off my arm, "Mmmm? Mmm?" she breathes and rolls to the side, facing away.

This room, shades drawn, my room, I see it in the partial light that leaks around the edges of the blinds.

My room. Not sand. Dark, almost dark. But no stars. There were stars.

Oh no, I sob to myself. I have lost everything. He has. I have. The dream just ended, and any certainty of who I am, now shredding like fog when the wind changes.

We were out alone, just our team. In this dream, I mean. I was him, the Marine. I was one of them. Between Heaven and Earth. There, right there, with them all, in the desert. I knew them. Like I really knew them, loved them. Between the life we all thought we had back in the world, and this, this ... what was surrounding us now. In all of it's quiet and deadly certainty. On the edges of the Wadi.

It was night, and I was noticing, couldn't help staring at, all the stars. So close. And not a twinkle. Some of the fellas were leaning against packs, some talking low and I could not hear what they were saying. I could feel the fear though, just like I could feel it in the jungle, long ago. Not a breath of wind, the sand-covered surface beneath us our nightly carpet.

"Fuck it, man," came from the one we call Benton. And the others made whispers too. Benton sat up, said something about never getting our own, and nobody asked what he meant.

Then he got ready to move out and croaked, "Who's with me?" And as we all shifted our gear,

Benton told me to stay if I knew what was good for me. Told me to keep it all to ourselves. Me and the other guy, WillieG. I heard myself talking him out of it, but it didn't work, and he and the rest were gone, smudged faces, silent footsteps, gone. He called me Birdman.

I was remembering, in this dream, that Benton had a thing about what he called "Permian Basins." How he would tell me, the Me in this dream, that a long time ago, the planet's crust had two fast moving chunks that somehow broke off and headed north, one to the North American plate and the other to Asia, right smack where we were sitting.

Then I was alone in the darkness, and they were all gone. Lost. There was shooting in the near distance, some explosions, more shooting, our rifles plus AK's. Then a lot of quiet. Cemetery quiet. Nobody came back.

And now the dream is gone too. And I feel so lost. What am I doing here? And how ...? I can't go to Ray anymore, even if he is dying – I can't prove he didn't do it.

And there's this growing pull from Vietnam, from Tuyet. Both of them, young and old. And the flag.

And Rena? Turned that way, she looks a lot younger. With the sheet low on her hips and one breast visible beneath her up raised arm, I feel a stirring again. In the dark, in the warm dark California night, her scent rising ... .

I slide myself to the edge of the bed, sit there. Wishing I could just smoke. Find something for myself in that smoke, find it and hold it. Before it all vanishes.

Like smoke.

31

CMC - San Luis Obispo
_/_/2007. The Present.

It's more now than just proving he didn't do it. Ray ... is more to me than that. Maybe there's something I need to hear from him. About me.

I leave the motel, Rena still sleeping – the day just beginning to dawn – I just get in my rental and drive to Ray, I think. Except ...

> *I am driving to Morro Rock.*
> *It's like someone else is driving. It's*
> *on the way to the prison, sort of, but*
> *not directly. It looks like I'm going*
> *right back to where Rena and I ... .*
> *I'm out of the car, walking. On*
> *the sand. Again. The sun just up*
> *across the broad Pacific.*
> *– Wait a minute. Across the*
> *Pacific? My head swims, feet falter,*
> *scuff sand ...*

Down the beach, I see my granddaughter Tuyet, gentle swells lapping around her bare feet. It is warm, too warm. And there are no birds to cry.

Ray walks beside me. We are near the farthest reach of the waves ourselves. It's like we've been walking here a long time, mostly quiet, but it's a good quiet. I see he is looking down the beach at her.

"Funny, isn't it," he says, with no laugh in his voice.

"What."

"You. Me. Her. Here, now?"

"Oh."

"'Oh'? What do you mean, 'oh'?"

I think about his question, if it is a question and not just a criticism. Maybe I am way ahead here. I mean, she told me first, right? I've thought about it so much since then. A granddaughter. But I guess it is all new to Ray. And he has his own way of taking it all in.

"Ok, yes. I mean yes, when was something like this – *this* – ever going to happen? To anybody, let alone you ... and me. When?"

He watches her. He says nothing.

I stop short. He goes on a step, then turns his head back to me.

"What's going on?"

He stops too. That face begins to radiate humor. "Did you ever consider that, in the scheme of the last 300-600 million years of planetary evolution, we may all be no more than a rude smell?"

"You mean bad, and quickly gone?"

"Mm," is all he lets out as he turns again to look at Tuyet. Me too.

She stopped, when we did, but did not turn to look at us. Her vision seems directed far away, far out to sea. Then she turns her gaze on us. I feel that incredible pull, again.

"When we think about geological history," he says, looking at her looking at him, "when we think about it at all, we imagine it happening to an arrangement of continents that look like they do today. Same position relative to each other and to the poles and equator they have now. But it didn't happen that way," he turns to me, his face lit up. "All geological events – and for that matter all past animal events, all plant events and the great extinctions – all happened to continents shaped and spaced differently than they are today."

He turns and steps off down the beach toward her, his voice trailing over his shoulder, almost lost in the soft sounds of the eternal sea. "That was then. This is now."

*I watch him until he joins up
with Tuyet, his arm sliding easily
around her shoulders. A quick
freshet blows her hair up off her
cheek as she turns it to his face with a
smile wider than the dawn. And they
pass from my view ...*

... and I'm surrounded again by institutional walls – our visiting room, Ray just coming in the door. I may be imagining but his step seems to be just a little shorter, his frame a little more compact. He goes to his usual chair maybe just a little sooner. He waits, looks at me. No longer the angry push from his eyes. Maybe even ... a little invitation? He smiles, extends his palms out in a kind of universal, 'well?'

I feel stuck. What am I doing here? This time. Didn't I think he might have something to tell me? Has it all been said?

I sit down across from him, put my own palms together in front of me. Lean a little forward. Then, suddenly embarrassed, I straighten and lean back.

He brings his right hand up onto the table.

I look in his eyes. So much there to see, so much more behind all that. What time could there have been for us. Him and me. What might we have told each other, over the years.

I look away, to the high window and its bit of sky, ageless, and not passing.

"Do you ever think about your sister?" he asks me softly. "Eileen, isn't it? Youngest daughter of 11 kids, didn't you say?"

I look at him again. No, I didn't say. Or I don't remember that I did. When would I have said that?

"Does she write to you? Do you? Write to her?"

I think of Tuyet's words. *Paths you have taken together.*

He asks me even more softly, "Does she ever tell you about looking for her oldest brother? There on the ranch ... ?"

"*He is my grandfather ... ,*" she'd told me.

He smiles some more. "I'm not messin' with you, brother." He looks away, to that same window. That sky. He unfolds himself and walks slowly over to it, still looking out. Then turns to me. "It's been good. Your visits here. Whatever I first thought. Or said." He looks down a bit. "I guess," he chuckles, "I guess, I almost feel related to you."

I stand too. Nothing moves in the sky outside. Nothing moves in here either. Nothing anybody could see. I bring up a finger to one of my eyes. Turn a little away. "Yeah," I breathe quietly, "uh, me too."

We don't seem to have a goodbye thing going between us. Too hard to start now.

The table between us, him standing by the window. I turn to go. Then stop. 'Why not?' I think.

"So," I say, turning to face him. "*Did* you kill those two? In the jungle?"

Slowly he looks up into my face. He does not seem angry at my question this time, almost as if he had expected it, after all.

When I think he is not going to answer, I let my own gaze slip off his face, down his chest, to the floor, and again turn to go. When I think he is not going to answer, his voice comes, "If I tell you no?"

I look into his eyes to see what truth is there.

"You might believe me. But that wouldn't mean I didn't do it."

I don't know what to think. Why won't he just say 'No. I didn't. I did not kill those men.'

"Why won't you just say it!"

"Do you think I did?" He smiles. "So many men had already died, so many of us. Those two men were going to die too. Surely anybody would've done it, even you."

"What?" I am incredulous.

"Do you think I did it?"

"You? No. OK? I don't."

Something else passes across his face. Relief, I think. A little. And maybe some kind of fond regard. Brief. His eyes dark, deep, intent on me.

"Remember what we said about an acquittal? It doesn't mean I didn't do it."

I feel like I've been hit in the face with a brick. I feel flame and steel course down my arms to my fingertips.

"Goddamnit Clayton! Stop it! You don't belong here!

"I *always* belonged here!" he explodes.

I stand. Every muscle tight.

Then quietly, almost sympathetically, he goes on, "I was always gonna get here. All those years I lived on the streets? A burden and an embarrassment to my family? That was not my life. My life ended in the White Man's dungeons – I was robbed of it by a stupid – a brutal and stupid – military machine. And by white hatred.

"Yes, I was acquitted. Do you know what that means? It does not proclaim to the world that I did *not* do what I was accused of doing. It is a judicial fart. It only means that they couldn't *prove* that I did do it. Instead of a grand steaming movement produced for all the world to taste and see on the courtroom floor, what I got handed was a smear in the underpants of the seat of Justice!

"You think I wanted to be free? Well, maybe I did. But being turned out of the gates with their spittle on my cheeks? That was not my freedom. Not for me. Or my people – *this,*" he lifts his two hands palms up and gestures all around himself, including his whole life in this prison, and not just our small room, "this is my freedom."

I just let myself look at him, all of him, everything I can remember about him. Everything I think I have learned about him. From him. What he said on that beach about Tuyet, about geology. About "that was then … ."

We assume that all of our past happened to the person we are now. But no. It all happened to a long ago version of ourselves, before our own tectonic shifts brought us to where we are now.

32

Kontum Province, Vietnam
Near An Khe
_/_/2007. The Present.

Time.

We say that like everybody knows what we mean. It is time. Like something has just now arrived, but was not there before. Now. It is now.

But it is always now. And time is always there. I am the one who has arrived, the one who was not there before. I am the man, in the string of time, in its flow. And out of it. My time to finish what I started.

I got my papers in order, my passport, medical stuff. I used some more of my 'kill' money to buy an air ticket to Vietnam. I did not linger on the irony of paying my own way to a place I had prayed never to think of again, much less see, much less walk in.

All that is changed, now. I want to be here.
Not just for Ray.
Not because of the gravity of Tuyet's pull. Not just that.
I get it.

How I was ripped away from this place. So that I never really left. Not really. Never did 'go home'.

I landed at Tan Son Nhat International outside of Ho Chi Minh City (that I knew as Saigon), caught a connecting flight to Pleiku, then took a bus from the airport to An Khe and stayed the night there. The air was exactly the same as I remembered. Dense, impossibly dense. With time, with history. Centuries of bloody deeds. With the redolence of the ever-living jungle and the distant marshy plains. I slept only in fits that night. And dreamed. Saw the brown eyes again and again. But this time without the spark of violence that had always cast shadows in those dreams.

When I got up, I ate something quick and asked about finding my way out to the village. The one on the back of the flag.

I can't say it is beautiful here. The smells of rural life, the shapes, the land, the vegetation, even the animals, are all so alien to me. Old fears lurk just beneath every surface. Still, there is something here, in the air. Something besides heat and sweat, something out across the land. Serenity, I realize, with real shock. Serenity here? Where there was war? Impossible. But here it is.

Like nothing has happened here for a thousand years but the cycles of birth and death, seasons of growing and harvest. The land fertile, and at rest. I sit down, right down on the cart track I have been walking, the huts of the village just within sight.

I can hear the voices of its folk, and animal calls. The soughing of the gentle winds. I think maybe I will just sit here, and let this be my end. So different from the violent one I have always dreamed. Sit here and end my days? In this beauty?

My reverie is broken. I guess that sitting here, I have wandered far in time and space. But I kept no notes on these journeys.

Now the sun is low in the west, and I see two boys are standing at a respectful distance. Watching me. With brown eyes. Not the eyes of my dreams, no veiled wariness, no searching for advantage, for victory. Just the eyes of curious boys, perhaps in sight of a thing they had heard of but never imagined they would see. With those eyes.

"*Chao, cac ong,*" I greet them, in what I am sure is very bad, very rusty Vietnamese. Probably the wrong dialect for this village too.

The answering surprise in their faces is too much for me. I begin to laugh, as they pepper me with their own response, two intertwined and long strings of enthusiasm the only words of which I can make out are the last two from the older boy, "*Phai khong?*"

I hold my palms out and up, with raised shoulders and a small shake of my head in the universal gesture of, 'you got me there, pal.' I stutter out, "*Toi khong hieu – yi het!*" supposing I am telling them I cannot understand a word of it, but God only knows what they hear.

They turn toward each other in their hilarity and delight, and one shoves the other and they both race off, small clods flying from their sandaled feet.

I am thinking it is a sign for me to follow them, and I am just unfolding myself to stand, when a deep voice intones,"*Xin chao ong. Ong la ngoui ngai quoc. Lao lo khong gap ong.*" Or that's what it sounds like to me, except with much more music to it than my western ears can record. I turn slowly in the direction of the voice, and an old man, face wrinkled in smile, bows deeply to me. As his face comes into sight again, he smiles, "*Chao don tro lai.*" Then extends his hands toward me and his face becomes grave. "*Chao don nha.*"

I am totally lost, out of my depth. But it is not a bad feeling, and somehow I think I know his words are intended as a welcome. "I'm very sorry," I say, "I don't want to intrude, and I'm afraid I don't understand much of what you just said."

"Don't worry," he gives back, in serviceable English. "It is good that you are here." He begins to turn away from me toward the huts, and then extends one hand toward me slightly. "Will you come and have some tea? You must be tired and thirsty." He is waiting for me to join him. And I do.

He leads me up the steps of a hooch, not unlike those we'd used years before during the war. He notices me noticing and smiles, turning to me and saying, "We Viet people have always been resourceful, you know. In many places, a raised floor like this makes a big difference in how we live as a family, work together, share rice." He drops his eyes just slightly in polite deference, lets his smile dim just a bit as well.

"I did know that. Always admired that. How you could do so much, with so little."

His smile brightens and he sketches the briefest of head bows and turns to step across the threshold of the entrance to his hut. I can smell the warm sweet scent of rice slowly steaming.

One of his grandchildren I guess, or maybe a great-grandchild, a girl child, makes tea and pours some in small bowls for both of us, and I am almost transported back to Tuyet's tea ceremony. He is old enough, I find myself thinking. He could be her great-grandfather. A father-in-law I did not get to know.

We sip together for a long time while he tells me of his family, the ones now around us, working, playing, and the ones who have died, some a very long time ago, some not so long. His pride and, I think, his love for them all are evident in his speaking. And I realize it is beginning to seem like I know them. He speaks not at all about the war, or anything about the politics of his country. It is as if, to him, there has never been anything for his family but their life as a family in this land.

When he is finished with his tale, and the tea things have been cleared away, I sense it is my turn. He looks at me with polite expectance.

It feels awkward, I am unprepared. Reluctant. But I go ahead anyway. "You know, I came back to this place with a lot of fear. For me, it was a very bad time. In the war." I stop, caught in a cascade of images I thought were dead. Tuyet. Not my granddaughter, but the woman I thought I loved. No. I did love her. And I did leave her here. "There were moments I will always treasure," I tell the old man, and I tell myself. It is hard. It is terrible. I cannot hold her image in memory apart from my larger grim experience. "But I felt destroyed by the whole thing. I went home in a basket, for one thing." I wait to see how this is registering.

His look at me does not change that I can see. Somehow that helps me to continue.

"For many years, I would not let myself think about what happened. To me. To this place, to you. To my own country." Again I wait, and see. Still no change. "After I was wounded and sent home, my unit captured a flag. And they took it with them. I only found out about it recently, but I still feel responsible." The tale I was told of that capture slithers in my thoughts. I stop. He waits, and his waiting is like his breathing. Slow, unceasing, and with no other purpose.

I open my pack and take out the folded flag, look at it in my hands. For a moment, like a word too often repeated, it loses all meaning, context. An old rag in my hands. I hear myself saying, "I've brought it back with me. It belongs here." And I see my hands extend, with it, out toward him.

He looks only briefly at the folded object in my hands, then at me, at my face, my eyes. He stands up and walks to a far corner of the small hut. Then to a window and looks out, a long time. Eyes on some distant approach?

"The land here," he begins, still looking out the window, "has really never changed in all the years that my people have been on it. The marks that the last war made here are all gone. Erased by this land that claims us." Still his eyes, it seems, search impossible far reaches, and his ancient back, unbowed, is his face to me.

Then he slowly turns, without portent, as naturally as the rise of the evening breeze. "It is as if nothing of it ever happened." His eyes seem kind, or maybe I just need them to be. He holds my gaze, and in that holding I sense nothing. No malice, no accusation. It is just a holding. "And I think," he tells me, "it may be best to let the wisdom of the land guide us in this matter."

He steps to me and holds out both his hands. My own arms, still extended, finish their reach, leave the flag with him. I have a fleeting image of a movie scene where an honor guard hands the folded flag of a grateful nation to the father of a fallen son. But he stands with this flag in his hands, holding something precious, but not irreplaceable. There is no grief.

"We fought under this flag." In his face I think I see the faintest of smiles. "It is in many ways our heart." He looks down at what he holds, then back to me, "It is also our judge. We lost it, and that was somehow fitting. We continued to fight. Our land became whole again."

I slowly nod.

"Now?" he speaks to the bundle in his hand, "Will you come home now and be at rest? Let the land take you again to its breast?"

I get an idea that he is maybe also talking to me. I don't know. I feel it turning to conviction, I can't stop it. It makes no sense at all.

He turns and walks away from me to a chest on the floor, which he squats in front of and slowly opens. He unfolds the small square of cloth, looks at both sides, carefully, thoughtfully, then refolds it and lays it in the chest like putting an infant to bed.

When the lid of the chest is closed again, he turns, rising from his haunches, and stands suspended, looking at me. I do not know what to say. I had no plan for what to do or say beyond handing over the flag. I know now that no plan could have been useful.

Then a different grandchild brings us each a rice straw mat and sets them between us. "Would you join me for some rice?" The grandchild hovers waiting for my reply. When I say I would, gladly, the youngster goes off, and he continues, "I know you have been away a long time, and I would very much like to know where you went, and what you have made in the world. If it is not rude of me to ask?"

I am having that being-two-people sensation again, which I have been having now very often. One of me is perfectly aware that I have never been here, that I do not know this man at all, that his behavior toward me, while generous and kind, is completely unexplainable. The other of me is strangely at ease and enjoying the old man's attention. This is the me who answers, "Not at all. You have been very kind to me, a visiting stranger, *'ngoui nguai quoc'* I think you say. And an old enemy as well. *Phai khong?*"

This draws a hearty chuckle from him, as he bows slightly from the waist, "*Khong phai, tua ong.* Not so, honored guest. Many things have passed, many harms have brought their hurts to us, and to you. But our land, our Viet Hoa, has claimed you for its own." His face grows serious. "It no longer matters that you came to fight here, to kill. The land, our land, does not care." He is stillness, like the evening land beyond his window.

A strong wind, a gale, blows through me. History becomes fiction. I wait to see what comes next.

"You know this," he says. He turns to look out the window, away from me for a moment. He speaks to me as if I were outside, somewhere in the direction of his gaze. "You know this too. This is your land." Then turning back to me, with the clearest gaze I have ever seen, "You have come home. Let your family embrace you."

He says nothing more, gives no sign I can see, but the room fills with men and women, girls and boys, all of them speaking rapidly and with great animation. They surround us, hands touch my back as I sit, and everyone becomes silent. I am crying wordlessly, without tremor, without sound. Two streams of water down my face. All motion ceases then, as if there had never been any. As if time was being measured in the pace of continental movement.

And from behind the old man, and the family gathered around him, back by the trunk that now holds the flag, I see an image. Indistinct. Blurred, I think, by my tears. A woman. A young woman. Wearing a white *ao dai* and open-toed slippers, her hair dark and flowing back and then flipped over her right shoulder. And a boy. A boy whose hair is dark and short, his eyes the same color and almond-shaped. They both look at me steadily. With patience, waiting. Like they know me. Like I know what they want. I do. Though they seem hazy in the dim light of this space, they also have a light of their own. Warm, not stark. Translucent. Yes, I do know.

So my life here is endless. For a space.

"I have never left this land. Nor has anyone you see here." He looks around at them all. And at the pair of figures by the trunk behind him. Smiles at each of them, and as if that were instruction enough, they all move away and out of the hut, the light of the pair behind him dimming until there is only an afterimage of them in my eyes. One smallest boy child, maybe one of the two who I first saw, leaves his hand on my back to linger just a bit, and then he runs silently to join the others. "We have no idea what that would be like. You must tell me how that was for you."

Without any further thought about it, I do. I talk a long time and he never interrupts, never gives me less than his full attention. The rice, with a bit of vegetable and their pungent sauce, is served so I barely notice it. It is eaten with pleasure, and everything is cleared away. And I continue to talk. It has become dark. And I continue.

I do not remember now all that I said, or if I was careful to avoid any part of what I had thought of as my life. Even in the darkness, the liquid eyes of the old man watched me. I know I told him about Ray, Tuyet. Both grandmother and granddaughter. About the haunting boy. About my journeys to the desert and my strange younger self. About the years of anger and loss and my terrible dreams. And I told him all I knew about Eden.

And then I stop.

"Yes" is all he says for a long time. Then, "My people came here from the north, more than 10,000 years ago. To this land. Our land. *Viet Hoa*. "The Beautiful Country," in your language, though they would be the poorest of words. It is like nothing else.

And we are its people. And there has never been a time when others have not come to fight with us, to make themselves masters over us. But it cannot be. The land has claimed us. And it claims them too. We fight for a time, and then it is ended. For a while. I know the writings about your Eden. We think you would understand. You must ache so to return to that place. I have such compassion for a people so long apart from their paradise when I and my people have never left it."

The night sounds, the ones I once feared, even loathed, have risen. The humid breath of this land makes a bridge between our speaking lips.

• • •

They tell me that the Tigris and the Euphrates were long thought to be the cradle of civilization, the Fertile Crescent. Maybe even the Garden of Eden itself. If that is true, then the waters of those two rivers run from the mouth of that garden to this day, in a long exodus. And maybe the expulsion from the gate of that garden of the two creatures who dared to become aware of their choices also continues. Always cast out, never to be permitted a return.

Maybe all waters, no matter their origin, no matter where they rise, flow from that same garden. And all of us, lost to Eden, seek a return.

33

Iraq. Al Asad Airbase
_/_/2007. The Present.

It looks like they've moved me to division HQ while they prepare their case against me. I can't tell for sure because we got here at night. It looks like I am in the back of some local police station. Funny that. Feels a little like I've been here before. Not in this jail, but maybe in a jail somewhere before? My head feels really fuzzy when I try to remember. In fact, it feels like that when I try to remember anything before I got here. Oh man.

What about my parents. Sisters, brothers? Boot camp? I gotta remember boot camp – nobody ever forgets that. Maybe I'm cracking up. Did I kill Blake and Rivers and I just don't remember?

I can't say for sure anymore if I did it or not. I wanted to. Maybe that's the same thing. Maybe somebody just beat me to it.

I have a lot of time right now to think. Mostly there are no interruptions. I wonder about being trained to kill, about killing the enemy, trained about what's right and wrong in this war. And I wonder about meeting the enemy and then doing right by killing them. Except now they say it was wrong to kill these other men. Maybe it was wrong to send me and Benton and the others over here in the first place.

I think about my squad now, my buddies. How they are doing. I remember all of them. Even the ones I don't want to remember. I hate not being there with them. And yet, it feels like I am glad not to be in the fighting. Or rather the waiting. The terrible all-the-time alertness. Mostly for nothing. I am waiting now, but for this I do not have to be alert. I told them over and over I didn't do it, it wasn't me. I only took the rug. And I told them I'm not sorry those bastards got theirs. So, really, there's nothing else for me to do here. Just waiting.

I have time to wonder why I am here, behind the bars. Besides the murders and me being a suspect, I mean. Why suspect only me? There are lots of others – maybe everybody wanted Blake and Rivers dead. Is this some kind of Purpose at work here? I don't believe in that. Never did. Well, I think I never did, but now I can't remember.

Anyway, it wouldn't depend on my believing it, would it? I mean, if there is some kind of mystical purpose at work, why should it need my permission – why would anybody even let me in on it? It makes my head hurt worse. And I feel so tired now.

I'd like to get that rug back to the family. Now I don't know how. I imagine traveling out across the sands, like I did the first time, unwrapping it to lie in the cleansing and forgiving sun. Purification. Then, I don't know how, I would kneel on it, facing East? (Is that what they do here? Or is it West, because Mecca is not east from here?) And I would say a prayer.

"Allah walu Allah" I remember hearing this religious guy sing. There is no God but Allah. I think about this God of the Desert and its Rivers. They say that this was Eden. Once. Out there on that river.

Then I think about those strange dreams of mine, or whatever they are. The jungle, steaming with life. And death. Is there a God of Jungles and River Deltas? A different Eden?

Some say it's the same God. That we see God, or don't, based on our own differences, not on differences in God. Or Gods. They say.

And I've also heard that seeing no God at all – is like that too. I imagine God would have something to say about that. Maybe not.

I think of this Desert, where Paradise once was, I'm told. A Garden beyond my ability to imagine. A place, a life, we might never have left – have always longed to return to – but now lost. Denied, forever.

Is the Garden, like our Gods, only invisible because of how we look at things? How we see each other?

Is it right here, now? In front of me? Around me? Was I in a Garden when I fought and died as a soldier in the Jungle?

Did I miss it then, but now have another chance? And if I miss this one too, will there be another?
Allah walu Allah.

Yes. I would say a prayer for purification, for the rug, for me. Then I would roll it up, and carry it under my arm across the desert until I got to the river, and lay it down in the shallows of this Eden that was, and wash it and wash it. Until every last trace of us was gone from it. And then take it back. I cannot picture how I will be received.

I jump up off the cot, blood pounding the jazz into every muscle, my head spinning. That's rifle fire, and close by. The door between the cell area back here and the front crashes open, and a wounded officer falls through it and lands near my cell.

"Green on Blue!" he gurgles and spits up blood.

"Let me out of here! Give me a weapon!" I yell at him. I am near insane with a frenzy to fight. There's some fear in there too, I can tell. But I will die before I ever get shot if I have to stay in here while there's some kind of fight out front. "Let me out – I'm a Marine!"

The officer, a major I think, I cannot see his tabs with all the blood, looks at me, his eyes dimming. He coughs.

I pull myself together and stand tall and salute. "Marine to marine Sir, let me kill them for you."

I see his decision. He shoves himself over to the desk nearby, pulls out the ring of keys. Looks at me, measuring, coughs some more.

"Sir, there's no time," I manage, with what I hope is conviction and not panic.

He crawls to my door with determination, but his eyes go distant while he's trying to reach up with the key. I see him start to slump, and grab the keys from his relaxing fingers. Work the lock open myself, push the gate, and him with it, open enough to slip through, take his side arm, check the magazine and the load, cock the hammer and dive through the door.

Some while back, a bunch of the rebels figured out how to really mess with us. They'd steal uniforms, sometimes ours, sometimes some Coalition force, and mostly from the dead, or prisoners. And then show up at some HQ in the rear with dummy orders on paper that would fool somebody at a front desk just long enough to get that official boredom going and take their attention off the strangers for just a bit too long. And then they'd open up with everything they'd brought, suicidally charging through the building shooting everyone in sight. We called it "Green on Blue".

I rolled from my dive, the sound of semi- and full auto fire all around me. I shot the first guy I saw swinging his weapon around looking for targets. The officers and staff around me were either dead, knocked out, or returning fire from cover. But it was not good for them here. Against two maybe three fully armed fire teams, the fight with these side arms and few rifles in the hands of field grade officers and staff that were mostly not assault marines would not last long.

Another one burst into the room and I shot him too, rolled again to pick up a fallen rifle, checked the chamber and magazine too, and duck-walked in the direction of the most shooting, toward the front.

There I took a quick tally, saw there were maybe five running men all firing from the hip, several in similar uniforms already down and out, and maybe three of our HQ people still firing back from behind overturned desks that were not stopping much in the way of penetration. Before I could start firing again myself, a door to the side of the invaders slammed open and a Sergeant Major in full Class A's standing tall and filling the door shot two of them in quick succession, one shot each, before the rest got their weapons turned and knocked him down with automatic bursts. I shot them all before they finished with my rescuer.

I leaped across them checking to make sure they were dead, and checking the heroic senior staffer. He was gone too. I heard some cheers behind me as the other staffers began to stand up. "Stay down!" I yelled. "There's more of them out that way," I pointed. "Cover my rear," I ordered, and went out further front.

Shooting was sporadic. The murdering bastards were shooting the wounded. None of our people were still firing. There were two of the intruders. I shot one who was lining up on the head of a fallen woman, my vision blurred with blood and fury. The other guy dove to get behind an officer who was slumped against the front of a desk, arms limp, blood running down his face, but eyes still bright. My enemy wedged himself in behind his human shield, his weapon pointed at me, a fevered eye behind his sights. I took the time to aim, trying to spare the man he was hiding behind, and he shot me. Once. Before I blew his head off.

It's all quiet now. Everything has stopped. It feels like everything is slowing down. I feel like I'm sinking, through the floor. It is rising now, and soon it will be up to my chin. My lungs rattle with a thick congestion, hard to breathe. I cough and spit up blood down my front. Those bright eyes of the man I just saved are holding mine. "You did good, Marine," he breathes softly. Softly. So softly.

End of the Storm

Haboob.

I hear that's what desert people call it. It stretches along the bare western horizon as far as I can see in either direction north or south. This one is over a mile high and looks like an end-of-the-world disaster movie tidal wave.

It's not the first one I've seen coming across the sand, though maybe the largest since my tour here started. They can move at up to 60 miles per hour and when they hit, everything stops. You can't see. You can hardly breathe. And you sure as hell can't fly. We lost a big chopper over to the west of the province to one of these, I hear. Killed the engines and crashed it like a box of tools. Thirty good men and women died.

Even if you know you're safe inside a solid building your instincts still tell you to run, to haul ass. Your insides turn to water. People around you duck, or run out of the room.

This is the biggest thing I have ever had coming right at me.

And I am not in a building.

There are no buildings at all. None behind me, and nothing in front of me but desert. And it's a brown desert, not the kind I've just spent most of a year in — not the white stuff I can never get all the way off my skin and out of my lungs.

I am walking free, outside. Way outside. Just me and this churning wall of dirt. Not locked up in a cell. No battle torn room full of dead. Not dead myself, I guess.

I do think about running. About how I would not be able to run if I was inside. Inside where they were not even going to let me walk. And even if they would've let me run, I know I wouldn't have. It's just my guts want to run, and I know better.

You just can't outrun something this big. And there's something else I know. Or it feels like I know. Something buried down in with those other things I don't remember. Like my life before the desert. Like a dream I just had. The kind when I wake, all that's left is the reality of it, and none of the details.

I know I have seen this before, or something just like it. Not here, not in this desert. Not in this war. And we called it something else … .

• • •

I pull my bandana up over my nose and mouth, make my horse lie down behind some scrub and put my hat over its eyes. At the first rush of wind, I turn my own back, duck my head just a bit, before it hits us, hard enough to almost knock me over. Everything disappears. Even if I dared open my eyes, there would be nothing to see, not even parts of my body. My hand on the animal's neck feels its shiver, moves to dispel its fear. I make soft noises I know it cannot hear over the wind and the hiss of the dust, but which still reach it anyway. I can feel the nicker pulsing in its neck, the nervous movements of its hooves. We'll be alright, I think, sending this message to my friend, with easy strokes along its now dust-clogged fur.

We wait it out. Images, shapeless things move in my head. There is no sense of time in this tunnel, like it has blown away.

It gets gusty towards the end. That's how we know. Otherwise you can't tell how long they'll last. I check my watch, a little over 2 hours for this one. I brush myself off first, so when I stand I don't drop a great load of grit down my shirt and into my pants. I clear my face around my eyes the best I can before I open them, slap the bandanna and pull it loose and look around. I speak words of comfort to my mount, brush the dirt from around my hat, and lift it up and away from its eyes and let go of the lead at the same time so he knows its ok to get up. I step aside as its shaking creates its own dust storm aftermath. I put my hat back on my head and loosen the cinch on the saddle to clear the grit away from areas of pressure on the horse's ribs.

When we are done, I get back on, look around for orientation, head for the ranch. Birdland, my mother named it. A family joke, though humor's not what she intended, long ago when she was young and saw promise all around her.

As the ranch buildings come into view, I see ghostly overlays of mud, huts, barbed wire and gun emplacements sliding across my vision. A faint roar of jets overhead, a distant rolling boom of thunder. A reminder.

I take off a glove and wipe the sweat and dust from my eyes. Those images are gone, along with their sounds. But there are still more images in my head. War and fighting. But not images of jungle, no little brown men ... bright points of fire. These are hills of sand and white towns. Men with faces behind cloth, long dirt roads, exploding. Marines. Living and dead.

It makes my head swim, and I stop in my saddle, taking extra care not to fall off. There is a tightness in my head. Familiar and old. I wait it out.

I wait it out.

I feel my friend's long nicker in my thighs. He's anxious to get back for water and grain. And there she is. Eileen cantering toward me on her mare. Eileen, youngest of eleven ... my heart takes a leap of its own. I hold my breath, tall on my horse.

"Oh God," she says as she reins up, breathless. "I was worried! I saw that great duster towering in and we just got everything all shuttered up when I realized you were out there. In it!"

"No big deal," I hear myself say. And I realize that's true. It isn't. All in a day's work on the Birdland Ranch. Her ranch. Mine too, I realize, as if I had not known that before. "I'm tired. And hungry. I feel like I've been through the wars!" I kid her.

"Huh!" she returns, slapping her hat hard against my shoulder as she stands in the stirrups to reach across to me. Sending up a small echo of brown dust, an end to the storm.

And all I can picture in my head right now is what the supper table's gonna look like.

✳

CODA

Look.

Here is Charlie Bird.

And another Charlie Bird.

They are two men with the same name. Or are they the same man with two different histories? They both fight in a war, but not the same war.

Or is it.

One war is in the jungles of Southeast Asia, the other in the deserts of Iraq. One man fights in 1970, the other in 2007.

Two men are killed on a base in 1970. Two men are killed in a camp in 2007. Is it war, or murder?

Clayton Ray is accused of the 1970 deaths but acquitted. Then in 2007 he is in prison for a different crime. Charlie Bird in Iraq is accused of the 2007 deaths. And he does not remember if he did it or not.

Two ancient continental flakes rich in fossil deposits tear off and sail across the Earth's crust in different directions. One becomes the West Texas birthplace of Charles Bird, the other is buried under the sands on which the other Charles Bird fights and is perhaps condemned to die.

Oil is still King, and the powerful move armies as inexorably as the earth moves continents.

How is it that men hunger in secret for a return to a Garden, the paths to which were lost in the beginning, except for one – and that one now guarded by a flaming sword. Does every hero who endures the sword and the flames find the one true Garden? Or does he come upon some different Eden.

✻

Photo Credits

[upper left side, front cover] PF3650-VN5-0067a - SP5 Rick Parker, licensed, soldiers of US 4th Infantry Division (https://www.dotphoto.com/viewalbum.asp?AID=5325 534)

[upper right side, front cover] 050520-M-3643B-237 Al Anbar, Iraq (5/20/05) – Sgt Michael A. Blaha, public domain, US Marines prepare to leave Border Fort 12 via helicopter (https://commons.wikimedia.org/wiki/File:US-Marines -Iraq.jpg)

[upper center cover, composite]
Left   iStock 478690125 - PeopleImages (https://www.istockphoto.com/photo/He's-ready-for-w ar-gm478690125-36554364)
Right   iStock 163254441 - DanielBendjy (https://www.istockphoto.com/photo/american-soldier -portrait-gm163254441-23345739)
Center iStock 1087531642 - Victor Metelskiy (https://www.istockphoto.com/vector/man-avatar-profi le-male-face-silhouette-or-icon-isolated-on-white-backg round-vector-gm1142192548-306311139)

[back cover]
        istockphoto-483754751 Larry Herfindal, JungleBootsXXL (iStock-483754751.jpg)

[spine] photo portion of publisher's logo by Jan Watten, Jan Watten Studios, Alameda, CA

Acknowledgment

There are many, many people to whom I owe a debt of gratitude in making the telling of this story possible. Most of them have asked to remain anonymous.

From one particular disabled, distinguished Vietnam war medic, to a unit commander during the Iraq war, to men and women on the ground in both wars, Army and Marine; from a soldier accused and then acquitted of the deaths of other soldiers, to families of returning veterans and members of their communities; from a Navy trauma surgeon who barely slept while inventing new ways to save the lives of soldiers who would have simply died in any previous war, to hospital staff serving during and after the war; from readily available historical resources, to the many Vietnamese families who were gracious and generous with their time and understanding and their willingness to teach me about regional differences in heritage and language and about their long, long history and culture (they were even most patient with my slow learning of their language, and I apologize for any language errors of my own that may appear in the story).

I am also indebted to the many industry, military and government organizations and their employees whom I consulted over a long period of time.

My brother Dennis' example long ago, writing a major debut novel himself, was the implant deep in my unconscious of the idea that I too could write such a story. And, without my family, Helen and Christiann, Lauryth and Sara, my spouse Betty Jo (ever vigilant for any falling off in my inspiration to continue and to excel), my advance readers and my friends (you know who you are), I could not have completed this work.

Nor could I have done without the steadying influence of my two writing colleagues, Anne and Chris, who have shared with me their own paths to authorship. (And for anyone I have managed to overlook, I humbly apologize for the omission.)

I also give thanks to the major writing influences in my life, without whose tutelage and inspiration my work would be poorer in the outcome: Walter Mosley whose encouragements in his mentoring volume have kept me going, as well as Jorge Luis Borges and Ray Bradbury, James Lee Burke, Martin Cruz Smith, Junot Diaz, J. M. Coetzee, Elmore Leonard, Kurt Vonnegut, John Gardner and Mark Mustian.

My father, William R. "Bill" Dwyer, whose blood and epigenetics flow through my veins, came back from a war diminished in ways he never understood, and he was not understood by those who loved him. For him, there was no help. Today, and for many years now, those who have experienced life-altering trauma, in any of its many forms, do have resources, far better resources than I have fictionalized in my story. But such resources mean little to those who aren't aware of them, who may feel repelled by the idea of help, who are not embraced in some way by their families and communities and guided to seek out their own path to wholeness. Mighty men and women have been there for me all these years, through my own trials with a long-hidden, unknown and unremedied PTSD. And of course the work continues.

The opinions expressed here and in the story are mine, or are the product of my imagination in service to the story. They do not represent the views or policies of any person, organization, institution or government agency. Underlying facts used as inspiration have been researched to the best of my ability and to the extent of the publicly accessible resources. Any errors are entirely my own.

About the Author

Patrick Dwyer holds an MFA from UC Irvine and writes novels and short fiction from the Pacific Northwest. He has worked in a cold war embassy, in various research labs, on the Shakespearean stage and in the US Patent Office.

His short fiction has appeared in a number of anthologies, and he can be found on the publisher's website (icehousepress.com) as well as searched for on Amazon. This is his debut novel; he is working on his next one. About *The Silence at Sea* he writes,

> The Axis Powers seek world domination and in all the seas of the world the enemy prowls silently, deep beneath the waves. Two young brothers rush to enlist, each bursting to serve with distinction, both enamored of a sea they know nothing of. They are both trained in the new art of SONAR detection, and separately assigned to duty in different oceans. One brother is on convoy escort duty in the North Atlantic and sees furious and appalling action. The other brother is assigned to the South Pacific. But try as he might, he is unable to get aboard a combat vessel to do the job for which he is trained, for which his longing only grows with each frustration. And always the Great Sea, in all of its depths, maintains for both men its silence, a silence full of sounds. And waiting.

A very short sample from the forthcoming book:

"... and it is as if the Sea hates the unnatural
touch of iron upon its breast, longs to sink
it, down deep, far beneath its quick surface,
to the silence only the depths can hold.
Strives with it, so long as it floats, hull
plates thrusting the Sea aside, while the
primordial waters work to twist and crush
men's metal impertinence."

Of his writings, he says, "What I want, and hope
for, is that the reader comes to suspect, to imagine, that
the Character has lived some part of that reader's life."